I0669225

Reprint Publishing

FOR PEOPLE WHO GO FOR ORIGINALS.

www.reprintpublishing.com

IN CAMP WITH A TIN SOLDIER.

JIMMIEBOY AND THE TIN SOLDIERS.   PAGE 21.

In Camp With A Tin Soldier

BY

JOHN KENDRICK BANGS

ILLUSTRATED BY

E. M. ASHE

NEW YORK

R. H. RUSSELL & SON

MDCCCXCII

TO
RUSSELL.

CHAPTER I.

THE START.

"BR-R-R-RUB-A-DUB-DUB! Br-r-r-rub-a-dub-a-dub-dub! Br-r-r-rub-adub-dub-a-dub-dub-a-dub-dub!"

"What's that?" cried Jimmieboy, rising from his pillow on the nursery couch, and looking about him, his eyes wide open with astonishment.

"What's what?" asked mamma, who was sitting near at hand, knitting a pair of socks for a small boy she knew who would shortly want them to keep his feet warm when he went off coasting with his papa.

"I thought I heard soldiers going by," returned Jimmieboy, climbing up on the window-sill and gazing anxiously up and down the street. "There were drums playing."

"I didn't hear them," said mamma. "I guess you imagined it. Better lie down again, Jimmie-

boy, and rest. You will be very tired when papa
gets home, and you know if you are tired you'll
have to go to bed instead of taking supper with
him, and that would be too bad on his birthday."

"Is papa really going to have a birthday
to-day?" queried the little fellow. "And a cake
with candles in it?"

"Yes," answered mamma. "Two cakes with
candles on them, I think," she added.

"What's he to have two cakes for? I had only
one," said Jimmieboy.

"One cake wouldn't be big enough to hold all
the candles," mamma answered. "You see, papa
is a few years older than you are—almost six
times as old to-day, and if he has a candle for
every year, he'll have to have two cakes to hold
them all."

"Is papa six years old to-day?" asked Jimmieboy, resuming his recumbent position on the pillow.

"Oh, indeed, yes, he's thirty," said mamma.

"How many is thirty?" asked Jimmieboy.

"Never mind, dearest," returned mamma, giving Jimmieboy a kiss. "Don't you bother about
that. Just close those little peepers and go to
sleep."

So Jimmieboy closed his eyes and lay very still for a few minutes. He was not sorry to do it, either, because he really was quite sleepy. He ought to have had his nap before luncheon, but his mamma had been so busy all the morning, making ready for his papa's birthday dinner, that she had forgotten to call him in from the playground, where he was so absorbed in the glorious sport of seesawing with his little friend from across the way that he never even thought of his nap. As many as five minutes must have slipped by before Jimmieboy opened his eyes again, and I doubt if he would have done so even then had he not heard repeated the unmistakable sounds of drums.

"I did hear 'em that time, mamma," he cried, starting up again and winking very hard, for the sand-man had left nearly a pint of sand in Jimmieboy's eyes. "I heard 'em plain as could be."

To this second statement of Jimmieboy's that he heard soldiers going by somewhere, there was no answer, for there was no one in the room to give him one. His mamma, supposing that he had finally fallen asleep, had tiptoed out of the room and was now down stairs, so that the little fellow found himself alone. As a rule he did not like to be alone, although he knew of no greater delight than that of conversing with himself, and he was on the point of running to the door to call to his mother to return, when his attention was arrested by some very curious goings-on in a favorite picture of his that hung directly over the fire-place.

This picture was not, under ordinary circumstances, what any one would call a lively picture—in fact, it was usually a very quiet one, representing a country lane shaded on either side by great oak-trees that towered up into the sky, their branches overhanging the road so as to form a leafy arch, through which only an occasional ray of the sun ever found its way. From one end to the other of this beautiful avenue there were no signs of life, save those which were presented by the green leaves of the trees themselves, and the purling brook, bordered by grasses and mosses.that was visible a short distance in; no houses or cows or men or children were there in sight. Indeed, had it not been for a faint glimmering of sunlight at the far end of the road, some persons might have thought it a rather gloomy scene, and I am not sure but that even Jimmieboy, had he not wondered what there could be beyond the forest, and around the turn which the road took at that other end, would have found the picture a little depressing. It was his interest in what might possibly lie beyond the point at which the picture seemed to stop that had made it so great a favorite with him, and he had frequently expressed a desire to take a stroll along that road, to fish in the little stream, and to explore the hidden country around the turn.

So great was his interest in it at one time, that Jimmieboy's papa, who was a great person for finding out things, promised to write to the man who had painted the picture and ask him all about the unseen land, so that his little son's curiosity might be satisfied, a promise which he must have kept, for some days later, on his return from business, he took a piece of paper from his pocket and gave it to Jimmieboy, saying that there was the artist's answer. Jimmieboy couldn't read it, of course, because at that time he had not even learned his letters, so he got his papa to do it for him, and they made the pleasing discovery that the artist was a poet as well as a painter, for the answer was all in rhyme. If I remember rightly, this is the way it read:

AROUND THE TURN.

Around the turn are kings and queens ;
Around the turn are dogs and cats ;
Around the turn are pease and beans,
And handsome light blue derby hats.

Around the turn are grizzly bears ;
Around the turn are hills and dales ;
Around the turn are mice and hares,
And cream and milk in wooden pails.

Indeed, you'll find there horses, pigs,
Great seas and cities you'll discern ;
All things, in fact, including figs,
For all the world lies round the turn.

This explanation was quite satisfactory to
Jimmieboy, although he was a little fearful as
to what might happen if the grizzly bears should
take it into their heads to come down into the
nursery and hug him, which was certainly not
an unlikely thing for them to do, for the mice
had come—he had seen them himself—and his
mamma had often said that he was a most
huggable little fellow.

Now there was undoubtedly some sign of life
down the road, for Jimmieboy could see it with
his own eyes. There was something moving
there, and that something was dressed in gay
colors, and in front of it was something else that
shone brightly as an occasional ray of the sun

shimmered through the trees and glistened upon it. In an instant all thought of his mamma had flown from his mind, so absorbed was he by the startling discovery he had made up there in the picture. To turn back from the door and walk over to the fire-place was the work of a moment, and to climb up on the fender and gaze into the picture occupied hardly more than another moment, and then Jimmieboy saw what it was that was moving down the road, and with delighted ears heard also what that other thing was that preceded the moving thing.

The first thing was a company of tin soldiers marching in perfect time, their colors flying and the captain on horseback; and the other thing in front was a full brass band, discoursing a most inspiring military march in a fashion that set Jimmieboy strutting about the nursery like a general.

As the little fellow strode around the room his step was suddenly arrested by a voice immediately at his feet.

"Hi, there, Jimmieboy!" it said. "Please be careful where you are walking. You nearly stepped on me that time."

Jimmieboy stopped short and looked down upon the floor.

"Hello!" he said. "What are you doing there, colonel?"—for it was none other than the colonel of the tin soldiers himself who had thus requested him to look out where he stepped.

"There's trouble on hand," said the colonel, climbing up on to a footstool so as to be nearer Jimmieboy's ear, for he did not wish to alarm everybody by shouting out the dreadful news he had to impart. Jimmieboy's mamma, for instance, was a timid little woman, and she would have been very much frightened if she had known what had happened. "There's a great deal of trouble on hand," the colonel repeated. "The Noah in your ark fell asleep last night before the animals had gone to bed, and while he was napping, the Parallelopipedon got loose, ate up the gingerbread monkey and four peppermint elephants, and escaped out of the back window to the woods. Noah didn't find it out until an hour ago, when he went to feed the elephants, and immediately he made the discovery word came from the Pannikins, who live around the turn there in the woods, that the Parallelopipedon had eaten the roof off their house, and was at the time the letter was written engaged in whittling down the fences with a jackknife, and rolling all the pumpkins down the mountain-

side into Tiddledywinkland, and ruining the
whole country. We have got to capture that
animal before breakfast. If we don't, there's
no telling what may happen. He might even
go so far as to come back, and that would be
horrible."

"I don't think I remember the Parawelopipedon," said Jimmieboy, pronouncing the animal's
name with some difficulty. "What kind of an
animal was that?"

"Oh, he's an awful animal," returned the
colonel. "I don't blame you for not remember-
ing him, though, because he is a hard animal to
remember. He is the only animal they had
like him in the ark. They couldn't find two of
his sort, and I rather guess they are glad they
couldn't, because his appetite is simply dreadful,
and the things he eats are most embarrassing.
He's the one your papa was telling you about last
night before you went to bed. Don't you remember the rhyme he told you—beginning this way:

> ' The Parallelopipedon
> I do not like, because
> He has so many, many sides,
> And ninety-seven claws'?"

"Oh, yes," replied Jimmieboy. "He is the
same animal that——

> ' Hasn't got a bit of sense,
>   Or feather to his name ;
> No eye, no ear with which to hear,
>   But gets there just the same.' "

"That's it! that's it!" cried the colonel. "And don't you remember,

> ' There's not a thing he will not eat,
>   From pie to sealing-wax,
> Although he shows a preference for
>   Red bricks and carpet tacks' ?"

"Yes, I remember that very well now," said Jimmieboy. "Wasn't there a verse about his color, too? Didn't it say:

> ' His color is a fearful one—
>   A combination hue
> Of yellow, green, and purple, mixed
>   With solferino blue'? "

"No; that was the Parallelogram," replied the colonel. "A Parallelopipedon is six times as bad as a Parallelogram. His color has a verse about it, though, that says:

> ' His hue is the most terrible
>   That ever man has seen ;
> 'Tis pink and saffron, blue and red,
>   Mixed up with apple green'."

"Dear me!" cried Jimmieboy. "And do you mean to say he's really got away?"

"I do, indeed," returned the colonel. "Got away, and Noah is glad of it, because he doesn't have to feed him any more. But it 'll never do to let him stay loose; he will do too much damage. Why, Jimmieboy, suppose he should overeat himself and die? He's the only one in the world, and we can't afford to lose an animal like that; besides, after he has ruined all the country around the turn, it's just as like as not he'll begin on the rest of the picture, and eat it all up, frame and all."

"My!" cried the little boy. "That would be terrible, wouldn't it! You are right—he must be captured. I have half a mind to go along with you and help."

"Half a mind isn't enough," retorted the colonel, shaking his head. "You can't go into the soldier business unless you have a whole mind—so good-by, Jimmieboy. I must be running along; and should I not return, as the poet says,

'Pray do not weep for me, my boy,
    But, as the years slip by,
Drop all your pennies in a bank—
    Brave soldiers never die ;
And some day I'll turn up again,
    Exalted, high in rank,
And possibly I'll find some use
    For that small sum in bank.'"

"I'm not going to stay here while you are fighting," said Jimmieboy, with a determined shake of his head. "I've got a whole mind to go with you, and a uniform to wear as well. But tell me, can I get up there on the road?"

"Certainly," said the colonel. "I'll show you how, only put on your uniform first. They won't let you go unless you are suitably dressed. Little boys, with striped trousers like yours, would be out of place, but with a uniform such as yours is, with real gold on the cap and brass buttons on the coat—well, I'm not sure but what they'll elect you water-carrier, or general, or something equally important."

So Jimmieboy hurried to his clothes-closet and quickly donned his military suit, and grasping his sword firmly by the hilt, cried out:

"Ready!"

"All right," said the colonel. "They are waiting for us. Close your eyes."

Jimmieboy did as he was told.

"One—two—three—eyes open!" cried the colonel.

Again Jimmieboy did as he was ordered, although he couldn't see why he should obey the colonel, who up to this afternoon had been entirely subject to his orders. He opened his eyes at the command, and, much to his surprise, found himself standing in the middle of that wooded road in the picture, beneath the arching trees, the leaves of which rustled softly as a sweet perfumed breeze blew through the branches. About him on every side were groups of tin soldiers talking excitedly about the escape of the devastating Parallelopipedon, every man of them armed to the teeth and eager for the colonel's command to start off on the search expedition. The band was playing merrily under the trees up the road near the little brook, and back in the direction from which he had come, through the heavy gilt frame, Jimmieboy could see the nursery just as he had left it, while before him lay the turn at the end of the wood and the unknown country now soon to be explored.

CHAPTER II.

FOR a few moments Jimmieboy was so over-come by the extreme novelty of his position that he could do nothing but wander in and out among the trees, wondering if he really was him-self, and whether the soldiers by whom he was surrounded were tin or creatures of flesh and blood. They certainly looked and acted like human beings, and they talked in a manner entirely different from what Jimmieboy was ac-customed to expect from the little pieces of painted tin he had so often played with on the nursery floor, but he very soon learned that they were tin, and not made up, like himself, of bone and sinew.

The manner of his discovery was this: One of the soldiers, in a very rash and fool-hardy fash-ion, tried to pick up a stone from the road to throw at a poor little zinc robin that was whist-ling in the trees above his head, and in bending over after the stone and then straightening him-

self up to take aim, he snapped himself into two
distinct pieces—as indeed would any other tin
soldier, however strong and well made, and of
course Jimmieboy was then able to see that the
band with whom he had for the moment cast his
fortunes were nothing more nor less than bits of
brittle tin, to whom in some mysterious way had
come life. The boy was pained to note the
destruction of the little man who had tried to
throw the stone at the robin, because he was
always sorry for everybody upon whom trouble
had come, but he was not, on the whole, surprised at the soldier's plight, for the simple reason that he had been taught that boys who
threw stones at the harmless little birds in the
trees were naughty and worthy of punishment,
and he could not see why a tin soldier should not
be punished for doing what a small boy of right
feelings would disdain to do.

After he had made up his mind that his companions were really of tin, he became a bit fearful as to his own make-up, and the question that
he now asked himself was, "Am I tin, too, or
what?" He was not long in answering this question to his own satisfaction, for after bending his
little fingers to and fro a dozen or more times,
he was relieved to discover that he had not

changed. The fingers did not snap off, as he had feared they might, and he was glad.

Barely had Jimmieboy satisfied himself on this point when a handsomely dressed soldier, on a blue lead horse, came galloping up, and cried out so loud that his voice echoed through the tall trees of the forest:

"Is General Jimmieboy here?"

"Jimmieboy is here," answered the little fellow. "I'm Jimmieboy, but I am no general."

"But you have on a general's uniform," said the soldier.

"Have I?" queried Jimmieboy, with a glance at his clothes. "Well, if 1 have, it's because they are the only soldier clothes I own."

"Well, I am very sorry," said the soldier on horseback, "but if you wear those clothes you've got to be general. It's a hard position to occupy, and of course you'd rather be a high-private or a member of the band, but as it is, there is no way out of it. If the clothes would fit any one else here, you might exchange with him; but they won't, I can tell that by looking at the yellow stripes on your trousers. The stripes alone are wider than any of our legs."

"Oh!" responded Jimmieboy, "I don't mind being general. I'd just as lief be a general as not; I know how to wave a sword and march ahead of the procession."

At this there was a roar of laughter from the soldiers.

"How queer!" said one.

"What an absurd idea!" cried another.

"Where did he ever get such notions as that?" said a third.

And then they all laughed again.

"I am afraid," said the soldier on horseback, with a kindly smile which won Jimmieboy's heart, "that you do not understand what the duties of a general are in this country. We aren't bound down by the notions of you nursery people, who seem to think that all a general is good for is to be stood up in front of a cannon loaded with beans, and knocked over half a dozen times in the course of a battle. Have you ever read those lines of High-private Tinsel in his little book, 'Poems in Pewter,' in which he tells of the trials of a general of the tin soldiers?"

"Of course I haven't," said Jimmieboy. "I can't read."

"Just the man for a general, if he can't read," said one of the soldiers. "He'll never know what the newspapers say of him."

"Well, I'll tell you the story," said the horse-

man, dismounting, and standing on a stump by
the road-side to give better effect to the poem,
which he recited as follows:

"THE TIN SOLDIER GENERAL.

> I walked one day
> Along the way
> That leads from camp to city ;
> And I espied
> At the road-side
> The hero of my ditty.

> His massive feet,
> In slippers neat,
> Were crossed in desperation ;
> And from his eyes
> Salt tears did rise
> In awful exudation."

"In what?" asked Jimmieboy, who was not
quite used to grown-up words like exudation.

"Quarts," replied the soldier, with a frown.
"Don't interrupt. This poem isn't good for much
unless it goes right through without a stop—like
an express train."

And then he resumed:

> "It filled my soul
> With horrid dole
> To see this wailing creature ;
> How tears did sweep,
> And furrow deep,
> Along his nasal feature!

My eyes grew dim
To look at him,
To see his tear-drops soiling
His necktie bold,
His trimmings gold,
And all his rich clothes spoiling ;

And so I stopped,
Beside him dropped,
And quoth, ' Wilt tell me, mortal,
Wherefore you sighed ? '
And he replied :
Wilt I ?   Well, I shouldst chortle.' "

"I don't know what chortle means," said Jim-mieboy.

"Neither do I," said the soldier. "But I guess the man who wrote the poem did, so it's all right, and we may safely go on to the next verse, which isn't very different in its verbiology—"

"Its wha-a-at?" cried a dozen tin soldiers at once.

"Gentlemen," said the declaiming soldier, severely, "there are some words in our language which no creature should be asked to utter more than once in a life-time, and that is one of them. I shall not endanger my oratorical welfare by speaking it again. Suffice it for me to say that if you want to use that word yourselves, you will find it in the dictionary somewhere under

F, or Z, or Ph, or some other letter which I cannot at this moment recall. But the poem goes
on to say:

> " Then as we sat
> The road-side at—
> His tears a moment quelling—
> In accents pale
> He told the tale
> Which I am also telling."

"Dear me!" said a little green corporal at Jimmieboy's side. "Hasn't he begun the story yet?"

"Yes, stupid," said a high-private. "Of course
he has; but it's one of those stories that take a
long time to begin, and never finish until the
very end."

"Oh yes, I know," said another. "It's a story
like one I heard of the other day. You can lay
it down whenever you want to, and be glad to
have the chance."

"That's it," said the high-private.

"I wish you fellows would keep still," said the
soldier who was reciting. "I ought to have been
a quarter of the way through the first half of that
poem by this time, and instead of that I'm only a
sixteenth of the way through the first eighth."

"You can't expect to go more than eight miles
an hour," said the corporal, "even in poetry like
that. It can't be done."

"But what happened?" asked Jimmieboy, who was quite interested to hear the rest of the poem.

"I'll have to tell you some other time, general," replied the soldier. "These tin warriors here haven't any manners. Some day, when you have time to spare, I'll tell you the rest of it, because I know you'll be glad to hear it."

"Yes, general," put in the corporal, with a laugh. "Some day when you have a year to spare get him to tell you the first twenty-seventh of the next ninety-sixth of it. It won't take him more than eleven months and thirty-two days to do it."

"Bah!" said the poetic soldier, mounting his horse and riding off with an angry flush on his cheek. "Some day, when I get promoted to the ranks, I'll get even with you."

"Who is he, anyhow?" asked Jimmieboy, as the soldier rode off.

"He's Major Blueface, and he has to look after the luggage," replied the corporal. "And as for that poem of his, Jimmieboy, I want to warn you. He has a printed copy of it that takes seven trunks to carry. He says it was written by High-private Tinsel, but that's all nonsense. He wrote it himself."

"Then I like it all the better," said Jimmieboy. "I always like what people I like write."

"There's no accounting for tastes," returned the corporal. "We don't any of us like the major. That's why we made him major. Looking after luggage is such awfully hard work, we didn't want to make any one else do it, and so we elected him."

"Why don't you like him?" asked Jimmieboy. "He seems to me to be a very nice soldier."

"That's just it," returned the corporal. "He's just the kind of soldier to please little boys like you, and he'd look perfectly splendid in a white and gold parlor like your mamma's, but in camp he's a terror. Keeps his boots shined up like a looking-glass; wears his Sunday uniform all the time; in fact, he has seven Sunday uniforms— one for each day of the week; and altogether he makes the rest of us feel so mean and cheap that we can't like him. He offered a prize once to the soldier who'd like him the best, and who do you think won it?"

"I don't know," said Jimmieboy. "Who?"

"He won it himself," retorted the corporal. "Nobody else tried. But you'd better go over to the colonel's quarters right away, Jimmieboy. You know he wants you."

"He hasn't sent for me, has he?" asked the boy.

"Of course he has. That's what the major came to tell you," answered the corporal.

"But he didn't say so," returned Jimmieboy.

"No, he never does what he is sent to do," explained the corporal. "That's how we know. If he had told you the colonel wanted you, we'd all know the colonel didn't want you. He's a queer bird, that major. He's so anxious to read his poem to somebody that he always forgets his orders, and when he does half remember what he is sent to do, we can tell what the orders are by what he doesn't say."

"I shouldn't think he'd be a good man to look after the luggage if he forgets everything that way," said Jimmieboy.

"That's just where he's great," returned the corporal. "For, don't you see, every man in the regiment wants to carry about three times as much luggage as he ought to, and the major makes it all right by forgetting two-thirds of it. Oh, there's no denying that he's one of the greatest luggage men there ever was; but you run along now, or the colonel may lose his temper, and that always delays things."

"I'm not afraid of the colonel," said Jimmieboy, bravely.

"Neither are we," said the corporal, in reply to this, "but we don't like to have our campaign delayed, and when the colonel loses his temper we have to wait and wait until he finds it again. Sometimes it takes him a whole week."

So Jimmieboy, wondering more and more at the singular habits of the tin soldiers, ran off in search of the colonel, whom he found sitting by the brook-side fishing, and surrounded by his staff.

"Hello!" said Jimmieboy, as he caught sight of the colonel. "Having any luck?"

"Lots," said the colonel. "Been here only five minutes, and I've caught three hickory twigs, a piece of wire, and one of the finest colds in my head I ever had."

"Good," said Jimmieboy, with a laugh. "But aren't there any fish there?"

"Plenty of 'em," answered the colonel. "But they're all so small I'd have to throw 'em back if I caught 'em. They know that well enough, and so save me trouble by not biting. But I say, I suppose you know we can't start this expedition without ammunition?"

"What's that?" queried Jimmieboy, to whom the word ammunition was entirely new.

"Ammunition? Why, that's stuff to load our

guns with," returned the colonel. "You must be a great general not to know that."

"You must excuse me," said Jimmieboy, with a blush. "There is a great deal that I don't know. I'm only five years old, and papa hasn't had time to tell me everything yet."

"Well, it's all right, anyhow," replied the colonel. "You'll learn a great deal in the next hundred years, so we won't criticise; but of course, you know, we can't go off without ammunition any more than a gun can. Now, as general of the forces, it is your duty to look about you and lay in the necessary supplies. For the guns we shall need about fourteen thousand rounds of preserved cherries, seventeen thousand rounds of pickled peaches for the cannon, and a hundred and sixty-two dozen cans of strawberry jam for me."

Jimmieboy's eyes grew so round and large as he listened to these words that the major turned pale.

"Then," continued the colonel, "we have to have powder and shell, of course. Perhaps four hundred and sixteen pounds of powdered sugar and ninety-seven barrels of shells with almonds in 'em would do for our purposes."

"But—but what are we to do with all these

things, and where am I to get them?" gasped Jimmieboy, beginning to be very sorry that he had
accepted so important a position as that of general.

"Do with 'em?" cried the colonel. "What 'll
we do with 'em? Why, capture the Parallelopipedon, of course. What did you suppose we'd do
with 'em—throw them at canary-birds?"

"You don't load guns with preserved cherries,
do you?" asked the boy.

"We don't, eh? Well, I just guess we do," returned the colonel. "And we load the cannon
with pickled peaches, and to keep me from de-
serting and going over to the enemy, they keep
me loaded to the muzzle with strawberry jam
from the time I start until we get back."

"You can't kill a Parawelopipedon with cherries and peaches, can you?" asked Jimmieboy.

"Not quite, but nearly," said the colonel. "We
never hit him with enough of them to kill him,
but just try to coax him with 'em, don't you see?
We don't do as you do in your country. We
don't shoot the enemy with lead bullets, and
try to kill him and make him unhappy. We
try to coax him back by shooting sweetmeats at
him, and if he won't be coaxed, we bombard him
with pickled peaches until they make him sick,
and then he has to surrender."

"It must be pretty fine to be an enemy," said Jimmieboy, smacking his lips as he thought of being bombarded with sweetmeats.

"It is," exclaimed the colonel, with enthusiasm. "It's so nice, that they have to do the right thing by me in the matter of jam to keep me from being an enemy myself."

"But what do I get?" returned Jimmieboy, who couldn't see why it would not be pleasant for him to be an enemy, and get all these delightful things.

"You? Why, you get the almonds and the powdered sugar and all the mince-pie you can eat—what more do you want?" said the colonel.

"Nothing," gasped Jimmieboy, overcome by the prospect. "I wouldn't mind being a general for a million years at that rate."

With which noble sentiment the little fellow touched his cap to the colonel, and set off, accompanied by a dozen soldiers, to find the cherries, the peaches, the almonds, and the powdered sugar.

CHAPTER III.

THE expedition under Jimmieboy's command had hardly been under way a quarter of an hour when the youthful general realized that the colonel had not told him where the cherries and peaches and other necessary supplies were to be found.

"Dear me," he said, stopping short in the road. "I don't know anything about this country, and I am sure I sha'n't be able to find all those good things—except in my mamma's pantry, and it would never do for me to take 'em from there. I might have to fight cook to get 'em, and that would be dreadful."

"Yes, it would," said Major Blueface, riding up as Jimmieboy spoke these words. "It would be terribly awful, for if you should fight with her now, she wouldn't make you a single pancake or pie or custard or anything after you got back."

"I'm glad you've come," said Jimmieboy, with a sigh of relief. "Perhaps you can tell me what I've got to do to get that ammu—that ammu— oh, that ammuknow, don't you?"

"Ammunition?" suggested the major.

"Yes, that's it," said Jimmieboy. "Could you tell me where to get it?"

"I could; but, really," returned the major, "I'm very much afraid I'd better not, unless you'll promise not to pay any attention to what I say."

"I don't see what good that would do," said Jimmieboy, a little surprised at the major's words. "What's the use of your saying anything, if I am not to pay any attention to you?"

"I'll tell you if you'll sit down a moment," was the major's reply, upon which he and Jimmieboy sat down on a log at the road-side.

The major then recited his story as follows:

"THE MAJOR'S MISFORTUNE.

When I was born, some years ago,
   The world was standing upside down;
Pekin was off in Mexico,
   And Paris stood near Germantown.

The moon likewise was out of gear.
   And shone most brilliantly by day;
The while the sun did not appear
   Until the moon had gone away.

Which was, you see, a very strange,
   Unhappy way of doing things,
And people did not like the change,
   Save clods who took the rank of kings.

For kings as well were going wrong,
   And 'stead of crowns wore beaver hats,
While those once mean and poor grew strong;
   The dogs e'en ran from mice and rats.

The Frenchman spoke the Spanish tongue,
   The Russian's words were Turkestan ;
And England's nerves were all unstrung
   By cockneys speaking Aryan.

Schools went to boys, and billie-goats
   Drove children harnessed up to carts.
The rivers flowed up hill, and oats
   Were fed to babies 'stead of tarts.

With things in this shape was I born.
   The stars were topsy-turvy all,
And hence it is my fate forlorn
   When things are short to call them tall ;

When things are black to call them white ;
   And if they're good to call them bad;
To say 'tis day when it is night ;
   To call an elephant a shad.

And when I say that this is this,
   That it is that you'll surely know ;
For truth's a thing I always miss,
   And what I say is never so."

"Poor fellow!" cried Jimmieboy. "How very
unpleasant! Is that really a true story?"

"No," returned the major, sadly. "It is not true."

And then Jimmieboy knew that it was true, and he felt very sorry for the major.

"Never mind, major," he said, tapping his companion affectionately on the shoulder. "I'll believe what you say if nobody else does."

"Oh, don't, don't! I beg of you, don't!" cried the major, anxiously. "I wouldn't have you do that for all the world. If you did, it would get us into all sorts of trouble. If I had thought you'd do that, I'd never have told you the story."

"Very well," said Jimmieboy, "then I won't. Only I should think you'd want to have somebody believe in you."

"Oh, you can believe in me all you want," returned the major. "I'm one of the finest fellows in the world, and worthy of anybody's friendship—and if anybody ought to know, Jimmieboy, I'm the one, for I know myself intimately. I've known myself ever since I was a little bit of a boy, and I can tell you if there's any man in the world who has a noble character and a good conscience and a heart in the right place, I'm him. It's only what I say you mustn't believe in. Remember that, and we shall be all right."

"All right," said Jimmieboy. "We'll do it that way. Now tell me what you don't know about finding preserved cherries and pickled peaches. We've got to lay in a very large supply of them, and I haven't the first idea how to get 'em."

"H'm! What I don't know about 'em would take a long time to tell," returned the major, with a shake of his head, "because there's so much of it. In the first place,

> "I do not know
> If cherries grow
> On trees, or roofs, or rocks;
> Or if they come
> In cans—ho-hum !—
> Or packed up in a box.
>
> Mayhap you'll find
> The proper kind
> Down where they sell red paint ;
> And then, you see,
> Oh, dear ! Ah, me !
> And then again you mayn't."

"That appears to settle the cherries," said Jimmieboy, somewhat impatiently, for it did seem to him that the major was wasting a great deal of valuable time.

"Oh, dear me, no!" ejaculated the major. "I could go on like that forever about cherries. For instance:

" You might perchance
Get some in France,
And some in Germany ;
A crate or two
In far Barboo,
And some in Labradee."

" Where's Labradee?" asked Jimmieboy.

" It's Labrador," said the major, with a smile; " but Labradee rhymes better with Germany, and as long as you know I'm not telling the truth, and are not likely to go there, it doesn't make any difference if I change it a little."

"That's so," said Jimmieboy, with a snicker. " But how about those peaches? Do you know anything that isn't so about them?"

"Oh, yes, lots," said the major.

" I know that when the peach is green,
And growing on the tree,
It's harder than a common bean,
And yellow as can be.

I know that if you eat a peach
That's just a bit too young,
A lesson strong the act will teach,
And leave your nerves unstrung.

And, furthermore, I know this fact:
The crop, however halo
In every year before 'tis packed,
Doth never fail to fail."

"That's very interesting," said Jimmieboy,

when the major had recited these lines, "but it doesn't help me a bit. What I want to know is how the pickled peaches are to be found, and where."

"Oh, that's it, is it?" said the major. "Well, it's easy enough to tell you that. First as to how you are to find them—this applies to huckleberries and daisies and fire-engines and everything else, just as well as it does to peaches, so you'd better listen. It's a very valuable thing to know.

‘ The way to find a pickled peach,
  A cow, or piece of pumpkin pie,
A simple lesson is to teach,
  As can be seen with half an eye.

Look up the road and down the road,
  Look North and South and East and West.
Let not a single episode
  Come in betwixt you and your quest.

Search morning, night, and afternoon,
  From Monday until Saturday ;
By light of sun and that of moon,
  Nor mind the troubles in your way.

And keep this up until you get
  The thing that you are looking for,
And then, of course, you need not fret
  About the matter any more."

"You are a great help," said Jimmieboy.

"Don't mention it, my dear boy," replied the

major, so pleased that he smiled and cracked some of the red enamel on his lips. "I like to be useful. It's almost as good as being youthful. In fact, to people who lisp and pronounce their esses as though they were teeaitches, it's quite the same. It was very easy to tell you how to find a pickled peach, but it's much harder to tell you where. In fact, I don't know that I can tell you where, but if I were not compelled to ignore the truth I should inform you at once that I haven't the slightest idea. But, of course, I can tell you where you might find them if they were there— which, of course, they aren't. For instance:

> " Pickled peaches might be found
> In the gold mines underground ;
>
> Pickled peaches might be seen
> Rolling down the Bowling Green ;
>
> Pickled peaches might spring up
> In a bed of custard cup ;
>
> Pickled peaches might sprout forth
> From an ice-cake in the North ;
>
> I have seen them in the South
> In a pickaninny's mouth ;
>
> I have seen them in the West
> Hid inside a cowboy's vest ;
>
> I have seen them in the East
> At a small boy's birthday feast ;

> Maybe, too, a few you'd see
> In the land of the Chinee ;
>
> And this statement broad I'll dare :
> You might find them anywhere."

"Thank you," said Jimmieboy. "I feel easier now that I know all this. I don't know what I should have done if I hadn't met you, major."

"It's very unkind of you to say so," said the major, very much pleased by Jimmieboy's appreciation. "Of course you know what I mean."

"Yes," answered Jimmieboy, "I do. Now I'll tell you what I think. I think pickled peaches come in cans and bottles."

> " Bottles and cans,
> Bottles and cans,
> When a man marries it ruins his plans,"

quoted the major. "I got married once," he added, "but I became a bachelor again right off. My wife wrote better poetry than I could, and I couldn't stand that, you know. That's how I came to be a soldier."

"That hasn't anything to do with the pickled peaches," said Jimmieboy, impatiently. "Now, unless I am very much mistaken, we can go to the grocery store and buy a few bottles."

"Ho!" jeered the major. "What's the use of

buying bottles when you're after pickled peaches?

> ' Of all the futile, futile things—
>   Remarked the Apogee—
> That is as truly futilest
>   As futilest can be.'

You never heard my poem on the Apogee, did you, Jimmieboy?"

"No. I never even heard of an Apogee. What is an Apogee, anyhow?" asked the boy.

"To give definitions isn't a part of my bargain," answered the major. "I haven't the slightest idea what an Apogee is. He may be a bird with a whole file of unpaid bills, for all I know, but I wrote a poem about him once that made another poet so jealous that he purposely caught a bad cold and sneezed his head off; and I don't blame him either, because it was a magnificent thing in its way. I'll tell it to you. Listen:

"THE APOGEE.

> The Apogee wept saline tears
>   Into the saline sea,
> To overhear two mutineers
>   Discuss their pedigree.
>   Said he :
> Of all the futile, futile things
>   That ever I did see.
> That is as truly futilest
>   As futilest can be.

He hied him thence to his hotel,
  And there it made him ill
To hear a pretty damosel
  A bass song try to trill.
             Said he :
Of all the futile, futile things—
  To say it I am free—
That is about the futilest
  That ever I did see.

He went from sea to mountain height,
  And there he heard a lad
Of sixty-eight compare the sight
  To other views he'd had ;
            And he
Remarked : Of all the futile things
  That ever came to me,
This is as futily futile
  As futile well can be.

Then in disgust he went back home,
  His door-bell rang all day,
But no one to the door did come :
  The butler'd gone away.
            Said he :
This is the strangest, queerest world
  That ever I did see.
It's two per cent. of earth, and nine-
  Ty-eight futility."

"Isn't that elegant?" added the major, when
he had finished.

"It sounds well," said Jimmieboy. "But what
does it mean? What's futile?"

"Futile? What does futile mean?" said the major, slowly. "Why, it's—it's a word, you know, and sort of stands for 'what's the use.'"

"Oh," replied Jimmieboy. "I see. To be futile means that you are wasting time, eh?"

"That's it," said the major. "I'm glad you said it and not I, because that makes it true. If I'd said it, it wouldn't have been so."

"Well, all I've got to say," said Jimmieboy, "is that if anybody ever came to me and asked me where he could find a futile person, I'd send him over to you. Here we've wasted nearly the whole afternoon and we haven't got a single thing. We haven't even talked of anything but peaches and cherries, and we've got to get jam and sugar and almonds yet."

Here the major smiled.

"It isn't any laughing matter," said Jimmieboy. "It's a very serious piece of business, in fact. Here's this Parawelopipedon going around ruining everything he can lay his claws on, and instead of helping me out of the fix I'm in, and starting the expedition off, you sit here and tell me about Apogees and other things I haven't time to hear about."

"I was only smiling to show how sorry I was," said the major, apologetically.

> " I always smile when I am sad,
>   And when I'm filled with glee
> A solitary tear-drop trick-
>   Les down the cheek of me."

"Oh, that's it," said Jimmieboy. "Well, let's stop fooling now and get those supplies."

"All right," assented the major. "Where are the soldiers who accompanied you? We'll give 'em their orders, and you'll have the supplies in no time."

"How's that?" queried Jimmieboy.

"Why, don't you see," said the major, "that's the nice thing about being a general. If you have to do something you don't know how to do, you command your men to go and do it. That lifts the responsibility from your shoulders to theirs. They don't dare disobey, and there you are."

"Good enough!" cried Jimmieboy, delighted to find so easy a way out of his troubles. "I'll give them their orders at once. I'll tell them to get the supplies. Will they surely do it?"

"They'll have to, or be put in the guard-house," returned the major. "And they don't like that, you know, because the guard-house hasn't any walls, and it's awfully draughty. But, as I said before, where are the soldiers?"

"Why!" said Jimmieboy, starting up and looking anxiously about him. "They've gone, haven't they?"

"They seem to have," said the major, putting his hand over his eyes and gazing up and down the road, upon which no sign of Jimmieboy's command was visible. "You ordered them to halt when you sat down here, didn't you?"

"No," said Jimmieboy, "I didn't."

"Then that accounts for it," returned the major, with a scornful glance at Jimmieboy. "They've gone on. They couldn't halt without orders, and they must be eight miles from here by this time."

"What 'll happen?" asked the boy, anxiously.

"What 'll happen?" echoed the major. "Why, they'll march on forever unless you get word to them to halt. You are a gay general, you are."

"But what's to be done?" asked Jimmieboy, growing tearful.

"There are only two things you can do. The earth is round, and in a few years they'll pass this way again, and then you can tell them to stop. That's one thing you can do. The second is to despatch me on horseback to overtake and tell them to keep right on. They'll know what you mean, and they'll halt and wait until you come up."

"That's the best plan," cried Jimmieboy, with a sigh of relief. "You hurry ahead and make them wait for me, and I'll come along as fast as I can."

So the major mounted his horse and galloped away, leaving Jimmieboy alone in the road, trudging manfully ahead as fast as his small legs could carry him.

THE PARALLELOPIPEDON AND THE MIRROR.   PAGE 54.

CHAPTER IV.

AS the noise made by the clattering hoofs of Major Blueface's horse grew fainter and fainter, and finally died away entirely in the distance, Jimmieboy was a little startled to hear something that sounded very like a hiss in the trees behind him. At first he thought it was the light breeze blowing through the branches, making the leaves rustle, but when it was repeated he stopped short in the road and glanced backward, grasping his sword as he did so.

"Hello there!" he cried. "Who are you, and what do you want?"

"Sh-sh-sh!" answered the mysterious something. "Don't talk so loud, general, the major may come back."

"What if he does?" said Jimmieboy. "I rather think I wish he would. I don't know whether or not I'm big enough not to be afraid of you. Can't you come out of the bushes and let me see you?"

"Not unless the major is out of sight," was the answer. "I can't stand the major; but you needn't be afraid of me. I wouldn't hurt you for all the world. I'm the enemy."

"The what?" cried Jimmieboy, aghast.

"I'm the enemy," replied the invisible object. "That's what I call myself when I'm with sensible people. Other people have a long name for me that I never could pronounce or spell. I'm the animal that got away."

"Not the Parallelopipedon?" said Jimmieboy.

"That's it! That's the name I can't pronounce," said the invisible animal. "I'm the Parallelandsoforth, and I've been trying to have an interview with you ever since I heard they'd made you general. The fact is, Jimmieboy, I am very anxious that you should succeed in capturing me, because I don't like it out here very much. The fences are the toughest eating I ever had, and I actually sprained my wisdom-tooth at breakfast this morning trying to bite a brown stone ball off the top of a gate post."

"But if you feel that way," said Jimmieboy, somewhat surprised at this unusual occurrence, "why don't you surrender?"

"Me?" cried the Parallelopipedon. "A Parallelandsoforth of my standing surrender right on

the eve of a battle that means all the sweetmeats
I can eat, and more too? I guess not."

"I wish I could see you," said Jimmieboy,
earnestly. "I don't like standing here talking
to a wee little voice with nothing to him. Why
don't you come out here where I can see you?"

"It's for your good, Jimmieboy; that's why I
stay in here. I am an awful spectacle. Why, it
puts me all in a tremble just to look at myself;
and if it affects me that way, just think how it
would be with you."

"I wouldn't be afraid," said Jimmieboy,
bravely.

"Yes, you would too," answered the Parallelopipedon. "You'd be so scared you couldn't
run, I am so ugly. Didn't the major tell you
that story about my reflection in the looking-
glass?"

"No," answered Jimmieboy. "He didn't say
anything about it."

"That's queer. The story is in rhyme, and the
major always tells everybody all the poetry he
knows," said the invisible enemy. "That's why
I never go near him. He has only enough to last
one year, and the second year he tells it all over
again. I'm surprised he never told you about
my reflection in the mirror, because it is one of

his worst, and he always likes them better than the others."

"I'll ask him to tell it to me next time I see him," said Jimmieboy, "unless you'll tell it to me now."

"I'd just as lief tell you," said the Parallelopipedon. "Only you mustn't laugh or cry, because you haven't time to laugh, and generals never cry. This is the way it goes:

"THE PARALLELOPIPEDON AND THE MIRROR.

The Parallelopipedon so very ugly is,
His own heart fills with terror when he looks upon his
    phiz.
That's why he wears blue goggles—twenty pairs upon his
    nose,
And never dares to show himself, no matter where he
    goes.

One day when he was walking down a crowded village
    street,
He looked into a little shop where stood a mirror neat.
He saw his own reflection there as plain as plain could be ;
And said, ' I'd give four dollars if that really wasn't me.'

And, strange to say, the figure in the mirror's silver face
Was also filled with terror at the other's lack of grace ;
And this reflection trembled till it strangely came to pass
The handsome mirror shivered to ten thousand bits of glass.

To this tale there's a moral, and that moral briefly is:
If you perchance are burdened with a terrifying phiz,
Don't look into your mirror—'tis a fearful risk to take—
'Tis certain sure to happen that the mirror it will break."

"Well, if that's so, I guess I don't want to see you," said Jimmieboy. "I only like pretty things. But tell me; if all this is true, how did the major come to say it? I thought he couldn't tell the truth."

"That's only as a rule. Rules have exceptions. For instance," explained the Parallelopipedon, "as a rule I can't pronounce my name, but in reciting that poem to you I did speak my name in the very first line—but if you only knew how it hurt me to do it! Oh dear me, how it hurt! Did you ever have a tooth pulled?"

"Once," said Jimmieboy, wincing at the remembrance of his painful experience.

"Well, pronouncing my name is to me worse than having all my teeth pulled and then put back again, and except when I get hold of a fine general like you I never make the sacrifice," said the Parallelopipedon. "But tell me, Jimmieboy, you are out after preserved cherries and pickled peaches, I understand?"

"Yes," said Jimmieboy. "And powdered sugar, almonds, jam, and several other things that are large and elegant."

"Well, just let me tell you one thing," said the Parallelopipedon, confidentially. "I'm so sick of cherries and peaches that I run every time I see them, and when I run there is no tin soldier or general of your size in the world that can catch me. Now what are we here for? I am here to be captured; you are here to capture me. To accomplish our various purposes we've got to begin right, and you might as well understand now as at any other time that you are beginning wrong."

"I don't know what else to do," said Jimmieboy. "I'm obeying orders. The colonel told me to get those things, and I supposed I ought to get 'em."

"It doesn't pay to suppose," said the Parallelopipedon. "Many a victory has been lost by a supposition. As that old idiot Major Blueface said once, when he tried to tell an untruth, and so hit the truth by mistake:

'Success always comes to
    The mortal who knows,
And never to him who
    Does naught but suppose.

For knowledge is certain,
    While hypothesees
Oft drop defeat's curtain
    On great victories.'"

"What are hypothesees?" asked Jimmieboy.

"They are ifs in words of four syllables," said the Parallelopipedon, "and you want to steer clear of them as much as you can."

"I'll try to," said Jimmieboy. "But how am I to get knowledge instead of hypothesecses? I have to take what people tell me. I don't know everything."

"Well, that's only natural," said the Parallelo-pipedon, kindly. "There are only two creatures about here that do know everything. They—between you and me—are me and myself. The others you meet here don't even begin to know everything, though they'll try to make you believe they do. Now I dare say that tin colonel of yours would try to make you believe that water is wet, and that fire is hot, and other things like that. Well, they are, but he doesn't know it. He only thinks it. He has put his hand into a pail of water and found out that it was wet, but he doesn't know why it is wet any more than he knows why fire is hot."

"Do you?" queried Jimmieboy.

"Certainly," returned the Parallelopipedon. "Water is wet because it is water, and fire is hot because it wouldn't be fire if it wasn't hot. Oh, it takes brains to know everything, Jimmieboy, and if there's one thing old Colonel Zinc hasn't got, it's brains. If you don't believe it, cut his head off some day and see for yourself. You won't find a whole brain in his head."

"It must be nice to know everything," said Jimmieboy.

"It's pretty nice," said the Parallelopipedon, cautiously. "But it's not always the nicest thing in the world. If you are off on a long journey, for instance, it's awfully hard work to carry all you know along with you. It has given me a headache many a time, I can tell you. Sometimes I wish I did like your papa, and kept all I know in books instead of in my head. It's a great deal better to do things that way; then, when you go travelling, and have to take what you know along with you, you can just pack it up in a trunk and make the railroad people carry it."

"Do you know what's going to happen to-morrow and the next day?" asked Jimmieboy, gazing in rapt admiration at the spot whence the voice proceeded.

"Yes, indeed. That's just where the great trouble comes in," answered the Parallelopipedon. "It isn't so much bother to know what has been—what everybody knows—but when you have to store up in your mind thousands and millions of things that aren't so now, but have got to be so some day, it's positively awful. Why, Jimmieboy," he said, impressively, "you'd be terrified if I told you what is going to be known by the time you go to school; it's awful to think of all the things you will have to learn then that aren't things yet, but are going to be within a year or two. I'm real sorry for the little boys who will live a hundred years from now, when I think of all the history they will have to learn when they go to school—history that isn't made yet. Just take the Presidents of the United States, for instance. In George Washington's time it didn't take a boy five seconds to learn the list of Presidents; but think of that list to-day! Why, there are twenty-five names on it now, and more to come. It gets harder every year. Now I—I know the names of all the Presidents there's ever going to be, and it would take me just eighteen million nine hundred and sixty-seven years, eleven months and twenty-six days, four hours and twenty-eight minutes to tell you all of them, and even then I wouldn't be half through."

"Why, it's terrible," said Jimmieboy.

"Yes, indeed it is," returned the Parallelopipedon. "You ought to be glad you are a little boy now instead of having to wait until then. The boys of the year 19,605,726,422 are going to have the hardest time in the world learning things, and I don't believe they'll get through going to school much before they're ninety years old."

"I guess the colonel is glad he doesn't know all that," said Jimmieboy, "if it's so hard to carry it around with you."

"Indeed he ought to be, if he isn't," ejaculated the Paralleopipedon. "There's no two ways about it; if he had the weight of one half of what I know on his shoulders, it would bend him in two and squash him into a piece of tin-foil."

"Say," said Jimmieboy, after a moment's pause. "I heard my papa say he thought I might be President of the United States some day. If you know all the names of the Presidents that are to come, tell me, will I be?"

"I don't remember any name like Jimmieboy on the list," said the Parallelopipedon; "but that doesn't prove anything. You might get elected on your last name. But don't let's talk about that—that's politics, and I don't like politics. What I want to know is, do you really want to capture me?"

"Yes, I do," said Jimmieboy.

"Then you'd better give up trying to get the peaches and cherries," said the Parallelopipedon, firmly. "I won't have 'em. You can shoot 'em at me at the rate of a can a minute for

ninety-seven years, and I'll never surrender.
I hate 'em."

"But what am I to do, then?" queried the little
general. "What must I do to capture you?"

"Get something in the place of the cherries
and peaches that I like, that's all. Very simple
matter, that."

"But I don't know what you like," said Jimmieboy. "I never took lunch with you."

"No—and you never will." answered the
Parallelopipedon. "And for a very good reason.
I never eat lunch, breakfast, tea, or supper. I
never eat anything but dinner, and I eat that
four times a day."

Jimmieboy laughed, half with mirth at the od-
dity of the Parallelopipedon's habit of eating,
and half with the pleasure it gave him to think of
what a delectable habit it was. Four dinners a
day seemed to him to be the height of bliss, and
he almost wished he too were a Parallelopipedon,
that he might enjoy the same privilege.

"Don't you ever eat between meals?" he asked,
after a minute of silence.

"Never," said the Parallelopipedon. "Never.
There isn't time for it in the first place, and in
the second there's never anything left between
meals for me to eat. But if you had ever dined

with me you'd know mighty well what I like,
for I always have the same thing at every single
dinner—two platefuls of each thing. It's a fine
plan, that of having the same dishes at every
dinner, day after day. Your stomach always
knows what to expect, and is ready for it, so
you don't get cholera morbus. If you want me
to, I'll tell you what I always have, and what you
must get me before you can coax me back."

"Thank you," said Jimmieboy. "I'll be very
much obliged."

And then the Parallelopipedon recited the following delicious bill of fare for the young
general.

"THE PARALLELOPIPEDON'S DINNER.

First bring on a spring mock-turtle
   Stuffed with chestnuts roasted through,
Served in gravy ; then a fertile
   Steaming bowl of oyster stew.

Then about six dozen tartlets
   Full of huckleberry jam,
Edges trimmed with juicy Bartletts—
   Pears, these latter—then some ham.

Follow these with cauliflower,
   Soaked in maple syrup sweet ;
Then an apple large and sour,
   And a rich red rosy beet.

Then eight quarts of cream—vanilla
  Is the flavor I like best—
Acts sublimely as a chiller,
  Gives your fevered system rest.

After this a pint of coffee,
  Forty jars of marmalade,
And a pound of peanut toffee,
  Then a pumpkin pie—home-made.

Top this off with pickled salmon,
  Cold roast beef, and eat it four
Times each day, and ghastly famine
  Ne'er will enter at your door."

"H'm! h'm! h'm!" cried Jimmieboy, dancing up and down, and clapping his hands with delight at the very thought of such a meal. "Do you mean to say that you eat that four times a day?"

"Yes," said the Parallelopipedon, "I do. In fact, general, it is that that has made me what I am. I was originally a Parallelogram, and I ate that four times a day, and it kept doubling me up until I became six Parallelograms as I am to-day. Get me those things—enough of them to enable me to have 'em five times a day, and I surrender. Without them, I go on and stay es, caped forever, and the longer I stay escaped, the worse it will be for these people who live about here, for I shall devastate the country. I shall

chew up all the mowing-machines in Pictureland. I'll bite the smoke-stack off every railway engine I encounter, and throw it into
the smoking car, where it really belongs. I'll
drink all the water in the wells. I'll pull up all
the cellars by the roots; I may even go so far as
to run down into your nursery, and gnaw into
the wire that holds this picture country upon
the wall, and let it drop into the water pitcher.
But, oh dear, there's the major coming down the
road!" he added, in a tone of alarm. "I must
go, or he'll insist on telling me a poem. But
remember what I say, my boy, and beware! I'll
do all I threaten to do if you don't do what I
tell you. Good-by!"

There was a slight rustling among the leaves,
and the Parallelopipedon's voice died away as
Major Blueface came galloping up astride of his
panting, lather-covered steed.

CHAPTER V.

THE MAJOR RETURNS.

"WELL," said Jimmieboy, as the major dismounted, "did you catch up with them?"

"No, I didn't," returned the major, evidently much excited. "I should have caught them but for a dreadful encounter I had up the road, for between you and me, Jimmieboy, I have had a terrible adventure since I saw you last, and the soldiers I went to order back have been destroyed to the very last man."

"Dear me!" cried Jimmieboy. "I am glad I didn't go with you. What happened?"

"I was attacked about four miles up the road by a tremendous sixty-pound Quandary, and I was nearly killed," said the major. "The soldiers had only got four and a half miles on their way, and hearing the disturbance and my cries for help they hastened to the rescue, and were simply an-ni-hi-lated, which is old English for all mashed to pieces."

"But how did you escape?" said the boy.

"Oh, I had a way, and it worked, that's all. I'm the safest soldier in the world, I am. You can capture me eight times a day, but I am always sure to escape," said the major, proudly. "But, my dear general, how is it that you do not tremble? Are you not aware that under the circumstances you ought to be a badly frightened warrior?"

"I don't tremble, because I don't know whether you are telling the truth or not," said Jimmieboy. "Besides, I never saw a Quandary, and so I can't tell how terrible he is. Is he dreadful?"

"He's more than dreadful," returned the major. "No word of two syllables expresses his dreadfulness. He is simply calamitous; and if there was a longer word in the dictionary applying to his case I'd use it, if it took all my front teeth out to say it."

"That's all very well," said Jimmieboy, "but you can't make me shiver with fear by saying he's calamitous. What does he do? Bite?"

"Bite? Well, I guess not," answered the major, scornfully. "He doesn't need to bite. Would you bite an apple if you could swallow it whole?"

"I think I would," said Jimmieboy. "How would I get the juice of it if I didn't?"

"You'd get just as much juice whether you bit it or not," snapped the major, who did not at all like Jimmieboy's coolness under the circumstances. "The Quandary doesn't bite anything, because his mouth is so large there isn't anything he can bite. He just takes you as you stand, gives a great gulp, and there you are."

"Where?" queried Jimmieboy, who could not quite follow the major.

"Wherever you happen to be, of course," said the major, gruffly. "You aren't a very sharp general, it seems to me. You don't seem to be able to see through a hole with a millstone in it. I have to explain everything to you just as if you were a baby or a school-teacher, but I can just tell you that if you ever were attacked by a Quandary you wouldn't like it much, and if he ever swallowed you you'd be a mighty lonesome general for a little while. You'd be a regular land Jonah."

"Don't get mad at me, major," said Jimmieboy, clapping his companion on the back. "I'll be frightened if you want me to. Br-rr-rrr-rrr-rrrrr! There, is that the kind of a tremble you want me to have?"

"Thank you, yes," the major replied, his face

clearing and his smile returning. "I am very
much obliged; and now to show you that you
haven't made any mistake in getting frightened,
I'll tell you what a Quandary is, and what he has
done, and how I managed to escape; and as
poetry is the easiest method for me to express
my thoughts with, I'll put it all in rhyme.

"THE QUANDARY.

He is a fearful animal,
  That quaint old Quandary—
A cousin of the tragical
And whimsically magical
  Dilemma-bird is he.

He has an eye that's wonderful—
  'Tis like a public school:
It has a thousand dutiful,
Though scarcely any beautiful,
  Small pupils 'neath its rule.

And every pupil—marvelous
  Indeed, sir, to relate—
When man becomes contiguous,
Makes certainty ambiguous—
  Which is unfortunate.

For when this ambiguity
  Has seized upon his prize,
Whate'er man tries, to do it he
Will find when he is through it, he
  Had best done otherwise.

And hence it is this animal,
  Of which I sing my song,
This creature reprehensible,
Is held by persons sensible
  Responsible for wrong.

So if a friend or foe you see
  Departing from his aim,
Be full, I pray, of charity—
He may have met the Quandary,
  And so is not to blame."

"That is very pretty," said Jimmieboy, as the major finished; "but, do you know, major, I don't understand one word of it."

Much to Jimmieboy's surprise the major was pleased at this remark.

"Thank you, Jimmieboy," he said. "That proves that I am a true poet. I think there's some meaning in those lines, but it's so long since I wrote them that I have forgotten exactly what I did mean, and it's that very thing that makes a poem out of the verses. Poetry is nothing but riddles in rhyme. You have to guess what is meant by the lines, and the harder that is, the greater the poem."

"But I don't see much use of it," said Jimmieboy. "Riddles are fun sometimes, but poetry isn't."

"That's very true," said the major "But poetry

has its uses. If it wasn't for poetry, the poets couldn't make a living, or if they did, they'd have to go into some other business, and most other businesses are crowded as it is."

"Do people ever make a living writing poetry?" Jimmieboy asked.

"Once in a while. I knew a man once who did. He called himself the Grocer-Poet, because he was a grocer in the day-time and a poet at night. He sold every poem he wrote, too," said the major.

"To a newspaper?" asked Jimmieboy.

"Oh, no," said the major. "He bought 'em from himself. When he'd wake up in the morning as a grocer he'd read what he had written the night before as a poet, and then he'd buy the verses from himself and throw them into the fire. But to return to the Quandary. He has awfully bad manners. He stares you right in the face whenever he meets you, and no matter what you want to do he tries to force you to do the other thing. The only way to escape him is not to do anything, but go back where you started from, and begin all over again."

"Where did you meet him?" asked Jimmieboy.

"Where? Why, where he's always met, of

course, at a fork in the road. That's where he gets in his fine work," said the major. "Suppose, for instance, you were out for a stroll, and you thought you'd like to go—well, say to Calcutta. You stroll along, and you stroll along, and you stroll along. Then you come to a place where the road splits, one half going to the right and one to the left, or, if you don't like right and left, we'll say one going to Calcutta by way of Cape Horn, and the other going to Calcutta by way of Greenland's icy mountains."

"It's a long walk either way," said Jimmieboy.

"Yes. It's a walk that isn't often taken," assented the major, with a knowing shake of the head. "But at the fork of this road the Quandary attacks you. He stops you and says, 'Which way are you going to Calcutta?' and you say, 'Well, as it is a warm day, I think I'll go by way of Greenland's icy mountains.' 'No,' says the Quandary, 'you won't do any such thing, because it may snow. You'd better go the other way.' 'Very well,' say you, 'I'll go the other way, then.' 'Why do you do that?' queries the Quandary. 'If it should grow very warm you'd be roasted to death.' 'Then I don't know what to do,' say you. 'What is the matter with going both ways?' says the Quandary, to which you reply, ' How can I do that?' ' Try it and see,' he answers. Then," continued the major, his voice sinking to a whisper—"then you do try it and you do see, unless you are a wise, sagacious, sapient, perspicacious, astute, canny, penetrating, needle-witted, learned man of wisdom like myself who knows a thing or two. In that case you don't try, for you can see without trying that any man with two legs who tries to walk along two roads leading in different directions at once is just going to split into at least two halves before he has gone twenty miles, and that is just what the Quandary wants you to do, for it's over such horrible spectacles as a man divided against himself that he gloats, and when he is through gloating he swallows what's left."

"And what does the wise, sagacious, sappy, perspiring man of wisdom like yourself who knows a thing or two do?" asked Jimmieboy.

"I didn't say sappy or perspiring," retorted the major. "I said sapient and perspicacious."

"Well, anyhow, what does he do?" asked Jimmieboy.

"He gives up going to Calcutta," observed the major.

"Oh, I see. To gain a victory over the Quan-

dary you turn and run away?" asked Jimmieboy.

"Yes, that's it. That's what saved me. I cried
for help, turned about, and ran back here, and I
can tell you it takes a brave man to turn his
back on an enemy," said the major.

"And why didn't the soldiers do it too?"
queried Jimmieboy.

"There wasn't anybody to order a retreat, so
when the Quandary attacked them they marched
right on, single file, and every one of 'em split
in two, fell in a heap, and died."

"But I should think you would have ordered
them to halt," insisted Jimmieboy.

"I had no power to do so," the major replied.
"If I had only had the power, I might have saved
their lives by ordering them to march two by
two instead of single file, and then when they
met the Quandary they could have gone right
ahead, the left-hand men taking the left-hand
road, the right-hand men the right, but of course
I only had orders to tell them to come back here,
and a soldier can only obey his orders. It was
awful the way those noble lives were sacrifi—"

Here Jimmieboy started to his feet with a cry
of alarm. There were unmistakable sounds of
approaching footsteps.

"Somebody or something is coming," he cried.

"Oh, no, I guess not," said the major, getting red in the face, for he recognized, as Jimmieboy did not, the firm, steady tread of the returning soldiers whom he had told Jimmieboy the Quandary had annihilated. "It's only the drum of your ear you hear," he added. "You know you have a drum in your ear, and every once in a while it begins its rub-a-dub-dub just like any other drum. Oh, no, you don't hear anybody coming. Let's take a walk into the forest here and see if we can't find a few pipe plants. I think I'd like to have a smoke."

"Why, you naughty major!" cried Jimmieboy, shaking his arm, which his companion had taken, free from the major's grasp. "You've been telling me a great big fib, because there are the soldiers coming back again."

"What!" ejaculated the major, in well-affected surprise. "Well, I declare! So they are. Dear me! Why, do you know, general, that is the most marvelous cure I ever saw in my life. To think that all those men whom I saw not an hour ago lying dead on the field of battle, all ready for the Quandary's luncheon, should have been resusticated in so short a time, as—"

"Halt!" roared Jimmieboy, interrupting the

major in a most unceremonious fashion, for the soldiers by this time had reached a point in the road directly opposite where he was sitting.

The soldiers halted.

"Break ranks!" cried Jimmieboy, after the corporal had told him the proper order to give next.

The soldiers broke ranks, and in sheer weariness threw themselves down on the soft turf at the side of the road—all except the corporal, who at Jimmieboy's request came and sat down at the general's side to make his report.

"This is fine weather we are having, corporal," said the major, winking at the subordinate officer, and trying to make him understand that the less he said about the major the better it would be for all concerned.

"Yes," returned the corporal. "Better for sleeping than for military duty, eh, major?"

Here the major grew pale, but had the presence of mind to remark that he thought it might rain in time for tea.

"There's something behind all this," thought Jimmieboy; "and I'm going to know what it all means."

Then he said aloud, "You have had a very speedy recovery, corporal."

Here the major cleared his throat more loudly than usual, blushed rosy red, and winked twice as violently at the corporal as before.

"Did you ever hear my poem on the 'Cold Tea River in China'?" he asked.

"No," said the corporal, "I never did, and I never want to."

"Then I will recite it for you," said the major.

"After the corporal has made his report, major," said Jimmieboy.

"It goes this way," continued the major, pretending not to hear.

" Some years ago—'way back in '69—a
   Friend and I went for a trip through China,
   That pleasant land where rules King Tommy Chang,
   Where flows the silver river Yangtse-Wang—
      Through fertile fields, through sweetest-scented bowers
      Of creeping vinous vines and floral flowers."

"My dear major," interrupted Jimmieboy, "I do not want to hurt your feelings, but much as I like to hear your poetry I must listen to the report of the corporal first."

"Oh, very well," returned the major, observing that the corporal had taken to his heels as soon as he had begun to recite. "Very well. Let the corporal proceed."

Jimmieboy then saw for the first time that the corporal had fled,

"Why, where is he?" he asked.

"I do not know," returned the major, coldly. "I fancy he has gone to the kitchen to cook his report. He always goes off when I recite."

"Oh, well, never mind," said Jimmieboy, noticing that the major was evidently very much hurt. "Go on with the poem about 'Cold Tea River.'"

"No, I shall not," replied the major. "I shall not do it for two reasons, general, unless you as my superior officer command me to do it, and I hope you will not. In the first place, you have publicly humiliated me in the presence of a tin corporal, an inferior in rank, and consequently have hurt my feelings more deeply than you imagine. I am not tall, sir, but my feelings are deep enough to be injured most deeply, and in view of that fact I prefer to say nothing more about that poem. The other reason is that there is really no such poem, because there is really no such a stream as Cold Tea River in China, though there might have been had Nature been as poetic and fanciful as I, for it is as easy to conceive of a river having its source in the land of the tea-trees, and having its waters so full of the essence of tea gained from contact with the roots of those trees, that to all intents and purposes it is a river of tea. Had you permitted me to go on uninterrupted I should have made up a poem on that subject, and might possibly by this time have had it done, but as it is, it never will be composed. If you will permit me I will take a horseback ride and see if I cannot forget the trials of this memorable day. If I return I shall be back, but otherwise you may never see me again. I feel so badly over your treatment of me that I may be rash enough to commit suicide by jumping into a smelting-pot and being moulded over again into a piece of shot, and if I do, general, if I do, and if I ever get into battle and am fired out of a gun, I shall seek out that corporal, and use my best efforts to amputate his head off so quickly that he won't know what has happened till he tries to think, and finds he hasn't anything to do it with."

Breathing which horrible threat, the major mounted his horse and galloped madly down the road, and Jimmieboy, not knowing whether to be sorry or amused, started on a search for the corporal in order that he might hear his report, and gain, if possible, some solution of the major's strange conduct.

CHAPTER VI.

JIMMIEBOY had not long to search for the corporal. He found that worthy in a very few minutes, lying fast asleep under a tree some twenty or thirty rods down the road, snoring away as if his life depended upon it. It was quite evident that the poor fellow was worn out with his exertions, and Jimmieboy respected his weariness, and restrained his strong impulse to awaken him.

His consideration for the tired soldier was not without its reward, for as Jimmieboy listened the corporal's snores took semblance to words, which, as he remembered them, the snores of his papa in the early morning had never done. Indeed, Jimmieboy and his small brother Russ were agreed on the one point that their father's snores were about the most uninteresting, uncalled for, unmeaning sounds in the world, which, no doubt, was why they made it a point to interrupt them on every possible occasion. The novelty of the present situation was delightful to the little general. To be able to stand there and comprehend what it was the corporal was snoring so vociferously, was most pleasing, and he was still further entertained to note that it was nothing less than a rollicking song that was having its sweetness wasted upon the desert air by the sleeping officer before him.

This is the song that Jimmieboy heard:

" I would not be a man of peace,
    Oh, no-ho-ho—not I;
But give me battles without cease ;
Give me grim war with no release,
    Or let me die-hi-hi.

I love the frightful things we eat
    In times of war-or-or ;
The biscuit tough, the granite meat,
And hard green apples are a treat
    Which I adore-dor-dor.

I love the sound of roaring guns
    Upon my e-e-ears,
I love in routs the lengthy runs,
I do not mind the stupid puns
    Of dull-ull grenadiers.

I should not weep to lose a limb,
    An arm, or thumb-bum-bum.
I laugh with glee to hear the zim
Of shells that make my chance seem slim
    Of getting safe back hum.

Just let me sniff gunpowder in
My nasal fee-a-ture,
And I will ever sing and grin.
To me sweet music is the din
Of war, you may be sure."

"Well, I declare!" cried Jimmieboy. "If my dear old papa could snore songs like that, wouldn't I let him sleep mornings!"

"He does," snored the corporal. "The only trouble is he doesn't snore as clearly as I do. It takes long practice to become a fluent snorer like myself—that is to say, a snorer who can be understood by any one whatever his age, nation, or position in life. That song I have just snored for you could be understood by a Zulu just as well as you understood it, because a snore is exactly the same in Zuluese as it is in your language or any other—in which respect it resembles a cup of coffee or a canary-bird."

"Are you still snoring, or is this English you are speaking?" asked Jimmieboy.

"Snoring; and that proves just what I said, for you understood me just as plainly as though I had spoken in English," returned the corporal, his eyes still tightly closed in sleep.

"Snore me another poem," said Jimmieboy.

"No, I won't do that; but if you wish me to I'll snore you a fairy tale," answered the corporal.

"That will be lovely," said Jimmieboy. "I love fairy tales."

"Very well," observed the corporal, turning over on his back and throwing his head back into an uncomfortable position so that he could snore more loudly. "Here goes. Once upon a time there was a small boy named Tom whose parents were so poor and so honest that they could not afford to give him money enough to go to the circus when it came to town, which made him very wretched and unhappy, because all the other little boys who lived thereabouts were more fortunately situated, and had bought tickets for the very first performance. Tom cried all night and went about the town moaning all day, for he did want to see the elephant whose picture was on the fences that could hold itself up on its hind tail; the man who could toss five-hundred-pound cannon balls in the air and catch them on top of his head as they came down; the trick horse that could jump over a fence forty feet high without disturbing the two-year-old wonder Pattycake who sat in a rocking-chair on his back. As Tom very well said, these were things one had to see to believe, and now they were coming, and just because he could not get fifty cents he could not see them.

"Then he thought, 'Here! why can't I go out into the world, and by hard work earn the fifty cents I so much need to take me through the doors of the circus tent into the presence of these marvelous creatures?'

"And he went out and called upon a great lawyer and asked him if he did not want a partner in his business for a day, but the lawyer only laughed and told him to go to the doctor and ask him. So Tom went to the doctor, and the doctor said he did not want a partner, but he did want a boy to take medicines for him and tell him what they tasted like, and he promised Tom fifty cents if he would be that boy for a day, and Tom said he would try.

"Then the doctor got out his medicine-chest and gave Tom twelve bottles of medicine, and told him to taste each one of them, and Tom tasted two of them, and decided that he would rather do without the circus than taste the rest, so the doctor bade him farewell, and Tom went to look for something else to do. As he walked disconsolately down the street and saw by the clock that it was nearly eleven o'clock, he made up his mind that he would think no more about the circus, but would go home and study arithmetic instead, the chance of his being able to earn the fifty cents seemed so very slight. So he turned back, and was about to go to his home, when he caught sight of another circus poster, which showed how the fiery, untamed giraffe caught cocoanuts in his mouth—the cocoanuts being fired out of a cannon set off by a clown who looked as if he could make a joke that would make an owl laugh. This was too much for Tom. He couldn't miss that without at least making one further effort to earn the money that would pay for his ticket.

"So off he started again in search of profitable employment. He had not gone far when he came to a crockery shop, and on stopping to look in the large shop window at the beautiful dishes and graceful soup tureens that were to be seen there. he saw a sign on which was written in great golden letters 'BOY WANTED.' Now Tom could not read, but something told him that that sign was a good omen for him, so he went into the shop and asked if they had any work that a boy of his size could do.

" 'Yes,' said the owner of the shop. 'We want an errand-boy. Are you an errand-boy?'

"Tom answered bravely that he thought he was, and the man said he would give him a trial anyhow, and sent him off on a sample errand, telling him that if he did that one properly, he would pay him fifty cent a day for as many days as he kept him, giving him a half holiday on all circus-days. Tom was delighted, and started off gleefully to perform the sample errand, which was to take a basketful of china plates to the house of a rich merchant who lived four miles back in the country. Bravely the little fellow plodded along until he came to the gate-way of the rich man's place, when so overcome was he with happmess at getting something to do that he could not wait to get the gate open, but leaped like a deer clear over the topmost pickets. But, alas! his very happiness was his ruin, for as he landed on the other side the china plates flew out of the basket in every direction, and falling on the hard gravel path were broken every one."

"Dear me!" cried Jimmieboy, sympathetically. "Poor little Tom."

> " Whereat the cow
>   Remarked, 'Pray how—
> If what you say is true—
>   How should the child,
>   However mild,
> Become so wildly blue ?' "

snored the corporal.

"What's the matter with you?" asked Jimmieboy, very much surprised at the rhyme, which, so far as he could see, had nothing to do with the fairy story.

"What's the matter with me?" returned the corporal. "Nothing. Why?"

"There wasn't anything about a cow in the fairy story you were telling about Tom," said Jimmieboy.

"Was I telling that story about Tom?" asked the sleeping soldier.

"Certainly," replied Jimmieboy.

"Then you must have interrupted me," snored the corporal. "You must never interrupt a person who is snoring until he gets through, because the chances are nine out of ten that, being asleep, he won't remember what he has been snoring about, and will go off on something else entirely. Where was I when you interrupted?"

"You had got to where Tom jumped over the gate and broke all the china plates," answered Jimmieboy.

"Very well, then. I'll go on, but don't you say another thing until I have finished," said the corporal. Then resuming his story, he snored away as foilows: "And falling on the hard gravel path the plates were broken every one, which was awfully sad, as any one could under-

TOM AND THE FAIRY GODMOTHER.   PAGE 87.

stand who could see how the poor little fellow
threw himself down on the grass and wept.
Dear me, how he wept! He wept so long and
such great tears, that the grass about him for
yards and yards looked as fresh and green as
though there had been a rain-storm.

"'Oh, dear! what shall I do?' cried Tom, rue-
fully regarding the shattered plates. 'They'll
beat me if I go back to the shop, and I'll never
get to see the circus after all.'

"'No,' said a voice. 'They will not beat you,
and I will see that you get to the circus.'

"'Who are you?' asked Tom, looking up and
seeing before him a beautiful lady, who looked
as if she might be a part of the circus herself.
'Are you the lady with the iron jaw or the horseback lady that jumps through hoops of fire?'

"'Neither,' replied the lady. 'I am your
Fairy Godmother, and I have come to tell you
that if you will gather up the broken plates and
take them up to the great house yonder, I will
fix it so that you can go to the circus.'

"'Won't they scold me for breaking the
plates?' asked Tom, his eyes brightening and his
tears drying.

"'Take them and see,' said the Fairy Godmother, and Tom, who was always an obedient

lad, did as he was told. He gathered up the broken plates, put them in his basket, and went up to the house.

"'Here are your plates,' he said, all of a tremble as he entered.

"'Let's see if any of them are broken,' said the merchant in a voice so gruff that Tom trembled all the harder. Surely he was now in worse trouble than ever.

"'H'm!' said the rich man taking one out and looking at it. 'That seems to be all right.'

"'Yes,' said Tom, meekly, surprised to note that the plate was as good as ever. 'It has been very neatly mended.'

"'Very what?' roared the rich man, who didn't want mended plates. 'Did you say mended?'

"'Oh, no, sir!' stammered Tom, who saw that he had made a bad mistake. 'That is, I didn't mean to say mended. I meant to say that they'd been very highly recommended.'

"'Oh! Recommended, eh?' returned the rich man more calmly. 'That's different. The rest of them seem to be all right, too. Here, take your basket and go along with you. Good-by!'

"And so Tom left the merchant's house very much pleased to have got out of his scrape so easily, and feeling very grateful to his Fairy Godmother for having helped him.

"'Well,' said she, when he got back to the gate where she was awaiting him, 'was everything all right?'

"'Yes,' said Tom, happily. 'The plates were all right, and now they are all left.'

"The Fairy Godmother laughed and said he was a bright boy, and then she asked him which he would rather do: pay fifty cents to go to the circus once, or wear the coat of invisibility and walk in and out as many times as he wanted to. To this Tom, who was a real boy, and preferred going to the circus six times to going only once, replied that as he was afraid he might lose the fifty cents he thought he would take the coat, though he also thought, he said, if his dear Fairy Godmother could find it in her heart to let him have both the coat and the fifty cents he could find use for them.

"At this the Fairy Godmother laughed again, and said she guessed he could, and, giving him two shining silver quarters and the coat of invisibility, she made a mysterious remark, which he could not understand, and disappeared. Tom kissed his hand toward the spot where she had stood, now vacant, and ran gleefully homeward, happy as a bird, for he had at last succeeded in obtaining the means for his visit to the circus. That night, so excited was he, he hardly slept a wink, and even when he did sleep, he dreamed of such unpleasant things as the bitter medicines of the doctor and the broken plates, so that it was just as well he should spend the greater part of the night awake.

"His excitement continued until the hour for going to the circus arrived, when he put on his coat of invisibility and started. To test the effect of the coat he approached one of his chums, who was standing in the middle of the long line of boys waiting for the doors to open, and tweaked his nose, deciding from the expression on his friend's face—one of astonishment, alarm, and mystification—that he really was invisible, and so, proceeding to the gates, he passed by the ticket-taker into the tent without interference from any one. It was simply lovely; all the seats in the place were unoccupied, and he could have his choice of them. Surely nobody could ask for anything better.

"You may be sure he chose one well down in front, so that he should miss no part of the performance, and then he waited for the beginning of the very wonderful series of things that were to come.

"Alas! poor Tom was again doomed to a very mortifying disappointment. He forgot that his invisibility made his lovely front seat appear to be unoccupied, and while he was looking off in another direction a great, heavy, fat man entered and sat down upon him, squeezing him so hard that he could scarcely breathe, and as for howling, that was altogether out of the question, and there through the whole performance the fat man sat, and the invisible Tom saw not one of the marvelous acts or the wonderful animals, and, what was worse, when a joke was got off he couldn't see whether it was by the clown or the ring-master, and so didn't know when to laugh even if he had wanted to. It was the most dreadful disappointment Tom ever had, and he went home crying, and spent the night groaning and moaning with sorrow.

"It was not until he began to dress for breakfast next morning, and his two beautiful quarters rolled out of his pocket on the floor, that he remembered he still had the means to go again. When he had made this discovery he became happy once more, and started off with his invisible coat hanging over his arm, and

paid his way in for the second and last performance like all the other boys. This time he saw
all there was to be seen, and was full of happiness, until the lions' cage was brought in, when
he thought it would be a fine thing to put on his
invisible coat, and enter the cage with the lion·
tamer, which he did, having so exciting a time
looking at the lions and keeping out of their
way that he forgot to watch the tamer when he
went out, so that finally when the circus was all
over Tom found himself locked in the cage with
the lions with nothing but raw meat to eat. This
was bad enough, but what was worse, the next
city in which the circus was to exhibit was hundreds of miles away from the town in which
Tom lived, and no one was expected to open the
cage doors again for four weeks.

"When Tom heard this he was frightened to
death almost, and rather than spend all that time
shut up in a small cage with the kings of the
beasts, he threw off the coat of invisibility and
shrieked, and then—"

"Yes—then what?" cried Jimmieboy, breath-
lessly, so excited that he could not help interrupting the corporal, despite the story-teller's
warning.

> " The bull-dog said he thought it might,
> But pussy she said ' Nay,'
> At which the unicorn took fright,
> And stole a bale of hay,"

snored the corporal with a yawn.

"That can't be it! that can't be it!" cried Jimmieboy, so excited to hear what happened to little Tom in the lions' cage that he began to shake the corporal almost fiercely.

"What can't be what?" asked the corporal, sitting up and opening his eyes. "What are you trying to talk about, general?"

"Tom—and the circus—what happened to him in the lions' cage when he took off his coat?" cried Jimmieboy.

"Tom? And the circus? I don't know anything about any Tom or any circus," replied the corporal, with a sleepy nod.

"But you've just been snoring to me about it," remonstrated Jimmieboy.

"Don't remember it at all," said the corporal. "I must have been asleep and dreamed it, or else you did, or maybe both of us did; but tell me, general, in confidence now, and don't ever tell anybody I asked you, have you such a thing as a—as a gum-drop in your pocket?"

And Jimmieboy was so put out with the cor-

poral for waking up just at the wrong time that
he wouldn't answer him, but turned on his heel,
and walked away very much concerned in his
mind as to the possible fate of poor little Tom.

CHAPTER VII.

A DISAGREEABLE PERSONAGE.

IT cannot be said that Jimmieboy was entirely happy after his falling out with the corporal. Of course it was very inconsiderate of the corporal to wake up at the most exciting period of his fairy story, and leave his commanding officer in a state of uncertainty as to the fate of little Tom; but as he walked along the road, and thought the matter all over, Jimmieboy reflected that after all he was himself as much to blame as the corporal. In the first place, he had interrupted him in his story at the point where it became most interesting, though warned in advance not to do so, and in the second, he had not fallen back upon his undoubted right as a general to command the corporal to go to sleep again, and to stay so until his little romance was finished to the satisfaction of his superior officer. The latter was without question the thing he should have done, and at first he thought he would go back and tell the corporal he was very sorry he hadn't done so. Indeed, he would have gone back had he not met, as he rounded the turn, a singular-looking little fellow, who, sitting high in an oak-tree at the side of the road, attracted his attention by winking at him. Ordinarily Jimmieboy would not have noticed anybody who winked at him, because his papa had told him that people who would wink would smoke a pipe, which was very wrong, particularly in people who were as small as this droll person in the tree. But the singular-looking little fellow winked aloud, and Jimmieboy could not help noticing him. Like most small boys Jimmieboy delighted in noises, especially noises that went off like pop-guns, which was just the kind of noise the tree dwarf made when he winked.

"Hello, you!" said Jimmieboy, as the sounds first attracted his attention. "What are you doing up there?"

"Sitting on a limb and counting the stars in the sky," answered the dwarf.

Jimmieboy laughed. This seemed such a curious thing to do.

"How many are there?" he asked.

"Seventeen," replied the dwarf.

"Ho!" jeered Jimmieboy.

"There are, really," said the dwarf. "I counted 'em myself."

"There's more than that," said Jimmieboy. "I've had stories told me of twenty-seven or twenty-eight."

"That doesn't prove anything," returned the dwarf, "that is, nothing but what I said. If there are twenty-eight there must be seventeen, so you can't catch me up on that."

"Come down," said Jimmieboy. "I want to see you."

"I can't come now," returned the dwarf. "I'm too busy counting the eighteenth star, but I'll drop my telescope and let you see me through that."

"I'll help you count the stars if you come," put in Jimmieboy. "How many stars can you count a day?"

"Oh, about one and a half," said the dwarf. "I could count more than that, only I'm cross-eyed and see double, so that after I've got through counting, I have to divide the whole number by two to get the proper figures, and I never was good at dividing. I've always hated division— particularly division of apples and peaches. There is no meaner sum in any arithmetic in the world

than that I used to have to do every time I go
an apple when I was your age."

"What was the sum?" asked Jimmieboy.

"It was to divide one apple by three boys,"
returned the queer little man. "Most generally
that would be regarded as a case of three into
one, but in this instance it was one into three;
and, worse than all, while it pretended to be division, and was as hard as division, as far as I
was concerned it was subtraction too, and I was
always the leftest part of the remainder."

"But I don't see why you had to divide your
apples every time you got any," said Jimmieboy.

"That's easy enough to explain," said the
dwarf. "If I didn't divide, and did eat the whole
apple, I'd have a fearful pain in my heart;
whereas if I gave my little brothers each a third,
it would often happen that they would get the
pain and not I. After one or two experiments
I fixed it so that I never got the pain part any
more—for you know every apple has an ache in
it—and they did. so, you see, I kept myself well
as could be, and at the same time built up quite
a reputation for generosity."

"How did you fix it so as to give them the pain
part always?" queried Jimmieboy.

"Why, I located the part of the apple that

held the pain. I did not divide one apple I got, but ate the whole thing myself, part by part. I studied each part carefully, and discovered that apples are divided by Nature into three parts, anyhow. Pleasure was one part, pain was another part, and the third part was just nothing—neither pleasure nor pain. The core is where the ache is, the crisp is where the pleasure is, and the skin represents the part which isn't anything. When I found that out I said, ' Here! What is a good enough plan for Nature is a good enough plan for me. I'll divide my apples on Nature's plan.' Which I did. To one brother I gave the core; to the other the skin; the rest I ate myself."

"It was very mean of you to make your brothers suffer the pain," said Jimmieboy.

"Well, they had their days off. One time one brother'd have the core; another time the other brother'd have it. They took turns," said the dwarf.

"It was mean, anyhow!" cried Jimmieboy, who was so fond of his own little brother that he would gladly have borne all his pains for him if it could have been arranged.

"Well, meanness is my business," said the dwarf.

"Your business?" echoed Jimmieboy, opening his eyes wide with astonishment, meanness seemed such a strange business.

"Certainly," returned the dwarf. "Don't you know what I am? I am an unfairy."

"What's that?" asked Jimmieboy.

"You know what a fairy is, don't you?" said the dwarf.

"Yes. It's a dear lovely creature with wings, that goes about doing good."

"That's right. An unfairy is just the opposite," explained the dwarf. "I go about doing unfair things. I am the fairy that makes things go wrong. When your hat blows off in the street the chances are that I have paid the bellows man, who works up all these big winds we have, to do it. If I see people having a good time on a picnic, I fly up to the sky and push a rain cloud over where they are and drench them, having first of course either hidden or punched great holes in their umbrellas. Oh, I can tell you, I am the meanest creature that ever was. Why, do you know what I did once in a country school?"

"No, I don't," said Jimmieboy, in tones of disgust. "I don't know anything about mean things."

"Well, you ought to know about this," returned

the dwarf, "because it was just the meanest thing anybody ever did. There was a boy who'd studied awfully hard in hopes that he would lead his class when the holidays came, and there was another boy in the school who was equal to him in everything but arithmetic, and who would have been beaten on that one point, so that the other boy would have stood where he wanted to, only I helped the second boy by rubbing out all the correct answers of the first boy and putting others on the slate instead, so that the first boy lost first place and had to take second. Wasn't that mean?"

"It was horrid," said Jimmieboy, "and it's a good thing you didn't come down here when I asked you to, for if you had, I think I should now be slapping you just as hard as I could."

"Another time," said the unfairy, ignoring Jimmieboy's remark, "I turned myself into a horse-fly and bothered a lame horse; then I changed into a bull-dog and barked all night under the window of a man who wanted to go to sleep, but my regular trick is going around to hat stores and taking the brushes and brushing all the beaver hats the wrong way. Sometimes when people get lost here in the woods and want to go to Tiddledywinkland, I give them the wrong directions, so that they bring up on the other side of the country, where they don't want to be; and once last winter I put rust on the runners of a little boy's sled so that he couldn't use it, and then when he'd spent three days getting them polished up, I pushed a warm rain cloud over the hill where the snow was and melted it all away. I hide toys I know children will be sure to want; I tear the most exciting pages out of books; I spill salt in the sugar-bowls and plant weeds in the gardens; I upset the ink on love-letters; when I find a man with only one collar I fray it at the edges I roll collar buttons under bureaus; I—"

"Don't you dare tell me another thing!" cried Jimmieboy, angrily. "I don't like you, and I won't listen to you any more."

"Oh, yes, you will," replied the unfairy. "I am just mean enough to make you, and I'll tell you why. I am very tired of my business, and I think if I tell you all the horrid things I do, maybe you'll tell me how I can keep from doing them. I have known you for a long time, only you didn't know it."

"I don't believe it," said Jimmieboy.

"Well, I have, just the same," returned the dwarf. "And I can prove it. Do you remember, one day you went out walking, how you walked two miles and only met one mud-puddle, and fell into that?"

"Yes, I do," said Jimmieboy, sadly. "I spoiled my new suit when I fell, and I never knew how I came to do it."

"I made you do that?" said the unfairy, triumphantly. "I grabbed hold of your foot, and upset you right into it. I waited two hours to do it, too."

"You did, eh?" said Jimmieboy. "Well, I wish I had an axe. I'd chop that tree down, and catch you and make you sorry for it."

"I am sorry for it," said the dwarf. "Real sorry. I've never ceased to regret it."

"Oh, well, I forgive you," said Jimmieboy, "if you are really sorry."

"Yes, I am," said the dwarf; "I'm awfully sorry, because I didn't do it right. You only ruined your suit and not that beautiful red necktie you had on. Next time I'll be more careful and spoil everything. But let me give you more proof that I've known you. Who do you suppose it was bent your railway tracks at Christmas so they wouldn't work?"

"You!" ejaculated Jimmieboy.

"Yes, sirree!" roared the dwarf. "I did, and,

what is more, it was I who chewed up your best
shoes and bit your plush dog's head off; it was
I who ate up your luncheon one day last March;
it was I who pawed up all the geraniums iu your
flower-bed; and it was I who nipped your friend
the postman in the leg on St. Valentine's day so
that he lost your valentine."

"I've caught you there," said Jimmieboy. "It
wasn't you that did those things at all. It was a
horrid little brown dog that used to play around
our house did all that."

"You think you are smart," laughed the
dwarf. "But you aren't. I was the little brown
dog."

"I don't see how you can have any friends if
that is the way you behave," said Jimmieboy,
after a minute or two of silence. "You don't
deserve any."

"No," said the dwarf, his voice trembling a
little—for as Jimmieboy peered up into the tree
at him he could see that he was crying just a bit—
"I haven't any, and I never had. I never had
anybody to set me a good example. My father
and my mother were unfairies before me, and I
just grew to be one like them. I didn't want to
be one, but I had to be; and really it wasn't until
I saw you pat a hand-organ monkey on the head,

instead of giving him a piece of cake with red pepper on it. as I would have done, that I ever even dreamed that there were kind people in the world. After I'd watched you for a while and had seen how happy you were, and how many friends you had, I began to see how it was that I was so miserable. I was miserable because I was mean, but nobody has ever told me how not to be mean, and I'm just real upset over it."

"Poor fellow!" said Jimmieboy, sympathetically. "I am really very, very sorry for you."

"So am I," sobbed the dwarf. "I wish you could help me."

"Perhaps I can," said Jimmieboy.

"Well, wait a minute," said the dwarf, drying his eyes and peering intently down the road. "Wait a minute. There is a sheep down the road there tangled up in the brambles. Wait until I change myself into a big black dog and scare her half to death."

"But that will be mean," returned Jimmieboy; "and if you want to change, and be good, and kind, why don't you begin now and help the sheep out?"

"H'm!" said the dwarf. "Now that is an idea, isn't it! Do you know, I'd never have thought of that if you hadn't suggested it to me. I think

I will. I'll change myself into a good-hearted shepherd's boy, and free that poor animal at once!"

The dwarf was as good as his word, and in a moment he came back, smiling as happily as though he had made a great fortune.

"Why, it's lovely to do a thing like that. Beautiful!" he said. "Do you know, Jimmieboy, I've half a mind to turn mean again for just a minute, and go back and frighten that sheep back into the bushes just for the bliss of helping her out once more."

"I wouldn't do that," said Jimmieboy, with a shake of his head. "I'd just change myself into a good fairy if I were you, and go about doing kind things. When you see people having a picnic, push the rain cloud away from them instead of over them. Do just the opposite from what you've been doing all along. and pretty soon you'll have heaps and heaps of friends."

"You are a wonderful boy," said the dwarf. "Why, you've hit without thinking a minute the plan I've been searching for for years and years and years, and I'll do just what you say. Watch!"

The dwarf pronounced one or two queer words the like of which Jimmieboy had never heard before, and, presto change! quick as a wink the unfairy had disappeared, and there stood at the small general's side the handsomest, sweetest little sprite he had ever even dreamed or read about. The sprite threw his arms about Jimmieboy's neck and kissed him affectionately, wiped a tear of joy from his eye, and then said:

"I am so glad I met you. You have taught me how to be happy, and I am sure I have lost eighteen hundred and seven tons in weight, I feel so light and gay; and—joy! oh, joy! I no longer see double! My eyes must be straight."

"They are," said Jimmieboy. "Straight as—straight as—well, as straight as your hair is curly."

And that was as good an illustration as he could have found, for the sprite's hair was just as curly as it could be.

CHAPTER VIII.

ARRANGEMENTS FOR A DUEL.

"WHERE are you going, Jimmieboy?" asked the sprite, after they had walked along in silence for a few minutes.

"I haven't the slightest idea," said Jimmieboy, with a short laugh. "I started out to provision the forces before pursuing the Parawelopipedon, but I seem to have fallen out with everybody who could show me where to go, and I am all at sea."

"Well, you haven't fallen out with me," said the sprite. "In fact, you've fallen in with me, so that you are on dry land again. I'll show you where to go, if you want me to."

"Then you know where I can find the candied cherries and other things that soldiers eat?" asked Jimmieboy.

"No, I don't know where you can find anything of the sort," returned the sprite. "But I do know that all things come to him who waits, so I'd advise you to wait until the candied cherries and so forth come to you."

"But what'll I do while I am waiting?" asked Jimmieboy, who had no wish to be idle in this new and strange country.

"Follow me, of course," said the sprite, "and I'll show you the most wonderful things you ever saw. I'll take you up to see old Fortyforefoot, the biggest giant in all the world; after that we'll stop in at Alltart's bakery and have lunch. It's a great bakery, Alltart's is. You just wish for any kind of cake in the world, and you have it in your mouth."

"Let's go there first, I'm afraid of giants," said Jimmieboy. "They eat little boys like me."

"Well, I don't blame them for that," said the sprite. "A little boy as sweet as you are is almost too good not to eat; but I'll take care of you. Fortyforefoot I haven't a doubt would like to eat both of us, but I have a way of getting the best of fellows of that sort, so if you'll come along you needn't have the slightest fear for your safety."

"All right," said Jimmieboy, after thinking it all over. "Go ahead. I'll follow you."

At this moment the galloping step of a horse

was heard approaching, and in a minute Major Blueface rode up.

"Why, how do you do, general?" he cried, his face beaming with pleasure as he reined in his steed and dismounted. "I haven't seen you in —my!—why, not in years, sir. How have you been?"

"Quite well," said Jimmieboy, with a smile, for the major amused him very much. "It doesn't seem more than five minutes since I saw you last," he added, with a sly wink at the sprite.

"Oh, it must be longer than that," said the major, gravely. "It must be at least ten, but they have seemed years to me—a seeming, sir, that is well summed up in that lovely poem a friend of mine wrote some time ago:

> "'When I have quarreled with a dear
> Old friend, a minute seems a year;
> And you'll remember without doubt
> That when we parted we fell out.'"

"Very pretty," said the sprite. "Very pretty, indeed. Reminds me of the poems of Major Blueface. You've heard of him, I suppose?"

"Yes," said the major, frowning at the sprite, whom he had never met before. "I have heard of Major Blueface, and not only have I heard of him, but I am also one of his warmest friends and admirers."

"Really?" said the sprite, not noticing apparently that Jimmieboy was nearly exploding with mirth. "How charming! What sort of a person is the major, sir?"

"Superb!" returned the major, his chest swelling with pride. "Brave as a lobster, witty as a porcupine, and handsome as a full-blown rose. In short, he is a wonder. Many a time have I been with him on the field of battle, where a man most truly shows what he is, and there it was, sir, that I learned to love and admire Major Blueface. Why, once I saw that man hit square in the back by the full charge of a brass cannon loaded to the muzzle with dried pease. The force of the blow was tremendous—forcible enough, sir, in fact, to knock the major off his feet, but he never quailed. He rose with dignity, and walked back to where the enemy was standing, and dared him to do it again, and when the enemy did it again, the major did not forget, as some soldiers would have done under the circumstances, that he was a gentleman, but he rose up a second time and thanked the enemy for his courtesy, which so won the enemy's heart that he surrendered at once."

"What a hero!" said the sprite.

"Hero is no name for it, sir. He is a whole history full of heroes. On another occasion which I recall," cried the major, with enthusiasm, "on another occasion he was pursued by a lion around a circular path—he is a magnificent runner, the major is—and he ran so much faster than the lion that he soon caught up with his pursuer from the rear, and with one blow of his sword severed the raging beast's tail from his body. Then he sat down and waited until the lion got around to him again, his appetite increased so by the exercise he had taken that he would have eaten anything, and then what do you suppose that brave soldier did?"

"What?" asked Jimmieboy, who had stopped laughing to listen.

"He gave the hungry creature his own tail to eat, and then went home," returned the major.

"Is that a true story?" asked the sprite.

"Do you think I would tell an untrue story?" asked the major, angrily.

"Not at all," said the sprite; "but if the major told it to you, it may have grown just a little bit every time you told it."

"No, sir. That could not be, for I am Major Blueface himself," interrupted the major.

"Then you are a brave man," said the sprite, "and I am proud to meet you."

"Thank you," said the major, his frown disappearing and his pleasant smile returning. "I have heard that remark before; but it is always pleasant to hear. But what are you doing now, general?" he added, turning and addressing Jimmieboy.

"I am still searching for the provisions, major," returned Jimmieboy. "The soldiers were so tired I hadn't the heart to command them to get them for me, as you said, so I am as badly off as ever."

"I think you need a rest," said the major, gravely; "and while it is extremely important that the forces should be provided with all the canned goods necessary to prolong their lives, the health of the commanding officer is also a most precious consideration. As commander-in-chief why don't you grant yourself a ten years' vacation on full pay, and at the end of that time return to the laborious work you have undertaken, refreshed?"

"But what becomes of the war?" asked Jimmieboy. "If I go off, there won't be any war."

"No, but what of it?" replied the major. "That 'll spite the enemy just as much as it will our side; and maybe he'll get so tired waiting for us to begin that he'll lie down and die or else give himself up."

"Well, I don't know what to do," said Jimmie-boy, very much perplexed. "What would you do?" he continued, addressing the sprite.

"I'd hire some one else to take my place if I were you, and let him do the fighting and provisioning until you are all ready," said the sprite.

"Yes, but whom can I hire?" asked the boy.

"The Giant Fortyforefoot," returned the sprite. "He'd be just the man. He's a great warrior in the first place and a great magician in the second. He can do the most wonderful tricks you ever saw in all your life. For instance,

> "He'll take two ordinary balls,
>   He'll toss 'em to the sky,
> And each when to the earth it falls
>   Will be a satin tie.
>
> He'll take a tricycle in hand,
>   He'll give the thing a heave,
> He'll mutter some queer sentence, and
>   'Twill go right up his sleeve.
>
> He'll ask you what your name may be,
>   And if you answer 'Jim !'
> He'll turn a handspring—one, two, three !
>   Your name will then be Tim.
>
> He'll take a fifty-dollar bill,
>   He'll tie it to a chain,
> He'll cry out 'Presto !' and you will
>   Not see your bill again."

MAJOR BLUEFACE AND THE SPRITE PREPARE LUNCH.   PAGE 120.

"I'd like to see him," said Jimmieboy. "But I can't say I want to be eaten up, you know, and I'd like to have you tell me before we go how you are going to prevent his eating me."

"Very proper," said Major Blueface. "You suffer under the great disadvantage of being a very toothsome, tender morsel, and in all probability Fortyforefoot would order you stewed in cream or made over into a tart. My!" added the major, smacking his lips so suggestively that Jimmieboy drew away from him, slightly alarmed. "Why, it makes my mouth water to think of a pudding made of you, with a touch of cinnamon and a dash of maple syrup, and a shake of sawdust and a hard sauce. Tlah!"

This last word of the major's was a sort of ecstatic cluck such as boys often make after having tasted something they are particularly fond of.

"What's the use of scaring the boy, Blueface?" said the sprite, angrily, as he noted Jimmieboy's alarm. "I won't have any more of that. You can be as brave and terrible as you please in the presence of your enemies, but in the presence of my friends you've got to behave yourself."

The major laughed heartily.

"Jimmieboy afraid of me?" he said. "Nonsense! Why, he could rout me with a frown. His little finger could, unaided, put me to flight if it felt so disposed. I was complimenting him— not trying to frighten him.

> " When I went into ecstasies
>   O'er pudding made of him,
> 'Twas just because I wished to please
>   The honorable Jim ;
> And now, in spite of your rebuff,
>   The statement I repeat :
> I think he's really good enough
>   For any one to eat."

"Well, that's different," said the sprite, accepting the major's statement. "I quite agree with you there; but when you go clucking around here like a hen who has just tasted the sweetest grain of corn she ever had, or like a boy after eating a plate of ice-cream, you're just a bit terrifying—particularly to the appetizing morsel that has given rise to those clucks. It's enough to make the stoutest heart quail."

"Nonsense!" retorted the major, with a wink at Jimmieboy. "Neither my manner nor the manner of any other being could make a stout hart quail, because stout harts are deer and quails are birds!"

This more or less feeble joke served to put the three travelers in good humor again. Jimmieboy smiled over it; the sprite snickered, and the major threw himself down on the grass in a perfect paroxysm of laughter. When he had finished lie got up again and said:

"Well, what are we going to do about it? I propose we attack Fortyforefoot unawares and tie his hands behind his back. Then Jimmieboy will be safe."

"You are a wonderfully wise person," retorted the sprite. "How on earth is Fortyforefoot to show his tricks if we tie his hands?"

"By means of his tricks," returned the major. "If he is any kind of a magician he'll get his hands free in less than a minute."

"Then why tie them at all?" asked the sprite.

"I'm not good at conundrums," said the major. "Why?"

"I'm sure I don't know," returned the sprite, impatiently.

"Then why waste time asking riddles to which you don't know the answer?" roared the major. "You'll have me mad in a minute, and when I'm mad woe be unto him which I'm angry at."

"Don't quarrel," said Jimmieboy, stepping between his two friends, with whom it seemed to be impossible to keep peace for any length of time. "If you quarrel I shall leave you both and go back to my company."

"Very well," returned the major. "I accept the sprite's apology. But he mustn't do it again. Now as you have chosen to reject my plan of attacking Fortyforefoot and tying his hands, suppose you suggest something better, Mr. Sprite."

"I think the safe thing would be for Jimmieboy to wear this invisible coat of mine when in the giant's presence. If Fortyforefoot can't see him he is safe," said the sprite.

"I don't see any invisible coat anywhere," said the major. "Where is it?"

"Nobody can see it, of course," said the sprite, scornfully "Do you know what invisible means?"

"Yes, I do," retorted the major. "I only pretended I didn't so that I could make you ask the question, which enables me to say that something invisible is something you can't see, like your jokes."

"I can make a better joke than you can with my hands tied behind my back," snapped the sprite.

"I can't make jokes with your hands tied behind your back, but I can make one with my own hands tied behind my back that Jimmieboy here can see with his eyes shut," said the major, scornfully.

"What is it? I like jokes," said Jimmieboy.

"Why—er—let me see; why—er—when is a sunbeam sharp?" asked the major, who did not expect to be taken up so quickly.

"I don't know; when?" asked Jimmieboy.

"When it's a ray, sir. See? Ray, sir—razor. Ha! ha! Pretty good, eh?" laughed the major.

"Bad as can be," said the sprite, his nose turned up until it interfered with his eyesight. "Now hear mine, Jimmieboy. When is a joke not a joke?"

"Haven't the slightest idea," observed Jimmieboy, after scratching his head and trying to think for a minute or two.

"When it's one of the major's," roared the sprite, whereat the woods rang with his laughter.

The major first turned pale and then grew red in the face.

"That settles it," he said, throwing off his coat. "That is a deadly insult, and there is now no possible way to avoid a duel."

"I am ready for you at any time," said the sprite, calmly. "Only as the challenged party I have the choice of weapons, and inasmuch as this is a hot day, I choose the jawbone."

"Not a talking match, I hope?" said the major, with a gesture of impatience.

"Not at all," replied the sprite. "A story-telling contest. We will withdraw to that moss-covered rock underneath the trees in there, gather enough huckleberries and birch bark for our luncheon, and catch a mess of trout from the brook to go with them, and then we can fight our duel all the rest of the afternoon."

"But how's that going to satisfy my wounded honor?" asked the major.

"I'll tell one story," said the sprite, "and you'll tell another, and when we are through, the one that Jimmieboy says has told the best story will be the victor. That is better than trying to hurt each other, I think."

"I think so too," put in Jimmieboy. "I'm ready for it."

"Well, it isn't a bad scheme," agreed the major. "Particularly the luncheon part of it; so you may count on me. I've got a story that will lift your hair right off your head."

So Jimmieboy and his two strange friends retired into the wood, gathered the huckleberries and birch bark, caught, cooked, and ate the trout, and then sat down together on the moss-covered rock to fight the duel. The two fighters drew lots to find out which should tell the first story, and as the sprite was the winner, he began.

And the story he told was as follows.

CHAPTER IX.

THE SPRITE'S STORY.

"WHEN I was not more than a thousand years old—" said the sprite.

"Excuse me," interrupted the major. "But what was the figure?"

"One thousand," returned the sprite. "That was nine thousand years ago—before this world was made. I celebrated my ten-thousand-and-sixteenth birthday last Friday—but that has nothing to do with my story. When I was not more than a thousand years of age, my parents, who occupied a small star about forty million miles from here, finding that my father could earn a better living if he were located nearer the moon, moved away from my birthplace and rented a good-sized, four-pronged star in the suburbs of the great orb of night. In the old star we were too far away from the markets for my father to sell the products of his farm for anything like what they cost him; freight charges were very

heavy, and often the stage-coach that ran between Twinkleville and the moon would not stop
at Twinkleville at all, and then all the stuff that
we had raised that week would get stale, lose its
fizz, and have to be thrown away."

"Let me beg your pardon again," put in the
major. "But what did you raise on your farm?
I never heard of farm products having fizz to
lose."

"We raised soda-water chiefly," returned the
sprite, amiably. "Soda-water and suspender buttons. The soda-water was cultivated and the
suspender buttons seemed to grow wild. We never knew exactly how; though from what I have
learned since about them, I think I begin to understand the science of it; and I wish now that
I could find a way to return to Twinkleville, because I am certain it must be a perfect treasure-
house of suspender buttons by this time. Even
in my day they used to lie about by the million—
metallic buttons every one of them. They must
be worth to-day at least a dollar a thousand."

"What is your idea about the way they happened to come there, based on what you have
learned since?" asked the major.

"Well, it is a very simple idea," returned the
sprite. "You know when a suspender button

comes off it always disappears. Of course it must go somewhere, but the question is, where ? No one has ever yet been known to recover the suspender button he has once really lost; and my notion of it is simply that the minute a metal suspender button comes off the clothes of anybody in all the whole universe, it immediately flies up through the air and space to Twinkleville, which is nothing more than a huge magnet, and lies there until somebody picks it up and tries to sell it. I remember as a boy sweeping our back yard clear of them one evening, and waking the next morning to find the whole place covered with them again ; but we never could make money on them, because the moon was our sole market, and only the best people of the moon ever used suspenders, and as these were unfortunately relatives of ours, we had to give them all the buttons they wanted for nothing, so that the button crops became rather an expense to us than otherwise. But with soda-water it was different. Everybody, it doesn't make any difference where he lives, likes soda-water, and it was an especially popular thing in the moon, where the plain water is always so full of fish that nobody can drink it. But as I said before, often the stage-coach wouldn't or couldn't stop, and we found ourselves getting poorer every day. Finally my father made up his mind to lease, and move into this new star, sink a half-dozen soda-water wells there, and by means of a patent he owned, which enabled him to give each well a separate and distinct flavor, drive everybody else out of the business."

"You don't happen to remember how that patent your father owned worked, do you?" asked the major, noticing that Jimmieboy seemed particularly interested when the sprite mentioned this. "If you do, I'd like to buy the plan of it from you and give it to Jimmieboy for a Christmas present, so that he can have soda-water wells in his own back yard at home."

"No, I can't remember anything about it," said the sprite. "Nine thousand years is a long time to remember things of that kind, though I don't think the scheme was a very hard one to work. For vanilla cream, it only required a well with plain soda-water in it with a quart of vanilla beans and three pints of cream poured into it four times a week; same way with other flavors—a quart of strawberries for strawberry, sarsaparilla for sarsaparilla, and so forth; but the secret was in the pouring; there was something in the way papa did the pouring; I never

knew just what it was. He always insisted
on doing the pouring himself. But if you don't
stop asking questions I'll never finish my story."

"You shouldn't make it so interesting if you
don't want us to have our curiosity excited by
it," said Jimmieboy. "I'd have asked those
questions if the major hadn't. But go ahead.
What happened?"

"Well, we moved, and in a very short time
were comfortably settled in the suburban star I
have mentioned," continued the sprite. "As we
expected, my father grew very, very rich. He
was referred to in the moon newspapers as 'The
Soda-water King,' and once an article about him
said that he owned the finest suspender-button
mine in the universe, which was more or less
true, but which, as it turned out, was unfortunate in its results. Some moon people hearing
of his ownership of the Twinkleville Button
Mines came to him and tried to persuade him
that they ought to be worked. Father said he
didn't see any use of it, because the common people didn't wear suspenders, and so didn't need the
buttons.

" 'True,' said they, 'but we can compel them to
need them, by making a law requiring that everybody over sixteen shall wear suspenders.'

"'That's a good idea,' said my father, and he tried to have it made a law that every one should wear suspenders, high or low, and as a result he got everybody mad at him. The best people were angry, because up to that time the wearing of suspenders had been regarded as a sign of noble birth, and if everybody, including the common people, were to have them they would cease to be so. The common people themselves were angry, because to have to buy suspenders would simply be an addition to the cost of living, and they hadn't any money to spare. In consequence we were cut off by the best people of the moon. Nobody ever came to see us except the very commonest kind of common people, and they came at night, and then only to drop pailfuls of cod-liver oil, squills, ipecac, and other unpopular things into our soda-water wells, so that in a very short time my poor father's soda-water business was utterly ruined. People don't like to order ten quarts of vanilla cream soda-water for Sunday dinner, and find it flavored with cod-liver oil, you know."

"Yes, I do know," said Jimmieboy, screwing his face up in an endeavor to give the major and the sprite some idea of how little he liked the taste of cod-liver oil. "I think cod-liver oil is

worse than measles or mumps, because you can't
have measles or mumps more than once, and
there isn't any end to the times you can have
cod-liver oil."

"I'm with you there," said the major, empha-
sizing his remark by slapping Jimmieboy on the
back "In fact, sir, on page 29 of my book called
'Musings on Medicines' you will find—if it is
ever published—these lines:

> " The oils of cod !
> The oils of cod !
> They make me feel tremendous odd,
> Nor hesitate
> I here to state
> I wildly hate the oils of cod. "

"Bravo!" cried the sprite. "When I start my
autograph album I want you to write those lines
on the first page."

"With pleasure," returned the major. "When
shall you start the album ?"

"Never, I hope," replied the sprite, with a
chuckle. "And now suppose you don't interrupt
my story again."

Clouds began to gather on the major's face
again. The sprite's rebuke had evidently made
him very angry.

"Sir," said he, as soon as his feelings permitted

him to speak. "If you make any more such re-
marks as that, another duel may be necessary
after this one is fought—which I should very
much regret, for duels of this sort consume a
great deal of time, and unless I am much mistaken it will shortly rain cats and dogs."

"It looks that way," said the sprite, "and it is
for that very reason that I do not wish to be
interrupted again. Of course ruin stared father
in the face."

"How rude of ruin!" whispered the major to
Jimmieboy, who immediately silenced him.

"Trade having fallen away," continued the
sprite, "we had to draw upon our savings for
our bread and butter, and finally, when the
last penny was spent, we made up our minds
to leave the moon district entirely and try life
on the dog-star, where, we were informed, people only had one eye apiece, and every man had
so much to do that it took all of his one eye's time
looking after his own business so that there wasn't
any left for him to spend on other people's business. It seemed to my father that in a place
like this there was a splendid opening for him."

"In what line?" queried the major.

"Renting out his extra eye to blind men,"
roared the sprite.

Jimmieboy fell off the rock with laughter, and the major, angry at being so neatly caught, rose up and walked away but immediately returned.

"If this wasn't a duel I wouldn't stay here another minute," he said. "But you can't put me to flight that way. Go on and finish."

"The question now came up as to how we should get to the dog-star," resumed the sprite. "Our money was all gone. Nobody would lend us any. Nobody would help us at all."

"I should think they'd have been so glad you were leaving they'd have paid your fare," said the major, but the sprite paid no attention.

"There was no regular stage line between the moon and the dog-star," said he, "and we had only two chances of really getting there, and they were both so slim you could count their ribs. One was by getting aboard the first comet that was going that way, and the other was by jumping. The trouble with the first chance was that as far as any one knew there wasn't a comet expected to go in the direction of the dog-star for eight million years—which was rather a long time for a starving family to wait, and besides we had read of so many accidents in the moon papers about people being injured while trying to board comets in motion that we were a

little timid about it. My father and I could have
managed very well; but mother might not have—
ladies can't even get on horse cars in motion
without getting hurt, you know.

"Then the other scheme was equally dangerous.
It's a pretty big jump from the moon to the dog-
star, and if you don't aim yourself right you are
apt to miss it, and either fall into space or land
somewhere else where you don't want to go.
For intance, a cousin of mine who lived on Mars
wanted to visit us when we lived at Twinkleville,
but he was too mean to pay his fare, thinking he
could jump it cheaper. Well, he jumped and
where do you suppose he landed?"

"In the sun!" cried the major, in horror.

"No. Nowhere!" returned the sprite. "He's
jumping yet. He didn't come anywhere near
Twinkleville, although he supposed that he was
aimed in the right direction."

"Will you tell me how you know he's falling
yet?" asked the major, who didn't seem to believe this part of the sprite's story.

"Certainly. I saw him yesterday through a
telescope," replied the sprite.

The major began to whistle.

"And he looked very tired, too," said the sprite.
"Though as a matter of fact he doesn't have to

exert himself any. All he has to do is fall, and, once you get started, falling is the easiest thing in the world. But of course with the remembrance of my cousin's mistake in our minds, we didn't care so much about making the jump, and we kept putting it off and putting it off until finally some wretched people had a law made abolishing us from the moon entirely, which meant that we had to leave inside of twenty-four hours; so we packed up our trunks with the few possessions we had left and threw them off toward the dog-star; then mother and father took hold of hands and jumped and I was to come along after them with some of the baggage that we hadn't got ready in time.

"According to my father's instructions I watched him carefully as he sped through space to see whether he had started right, and to my great joy I observed that he had—that very shortly both he and mother would arrive safely on the dog-star—but alas! My joy was soon turned to grief, for a terrible thing happened. Our great heavy family trunk that had been dispatched first, and with truest aim, landed on the head of the King of the dog-star, stove his crown in and nearly killed him. Hardly had the king risen up from the ground when he was again knocked

down by my poor father, who, utterly powerless
to slow up or switch himself to one side, landed
precisely as the trunk had landed on the monarch's head, doing quite as much more damage
as the trunk had done in the beginning. When
added to these mishaps a shower of hat-boxes
and hand-bags, marked with our family name,
fell upon the Lord Chief Justice, the Prime Minister and the Heir Apparent, my parents were
arrested and thrown into prison and I decided
that the dog-star was no place for me. Wild
with grief, and without looking to see where I
was going, nor in fact caring much, I gave a running leap out into space and finally through
some good fortune landed here on this earth
which I have found quite good enough for me
ever since."

Here the sprite paused and looked at Jimmieboy as much as to say, "How is that for a tale
of adventure?"

"Is that all?" queried Jimmieboy.

"Mercy!" cried the major, "Isn't it enough?"

"No," said Jimmieboy. "Not quite. I don't see
how he could have jumped so many years before
the world was made and yet land on the world."

"I was five thousand years on the jump,"
explained the sprite.

"It was leap-year when you started, wasn't it?" asked the major, with a sarcastic smile.

"And your parents? What finally became of them?" asked Jimmieboy, signaling the major to be quiet.

"I hadn't the heart to inquire. I am afraid they got into serious trouble. It's a very serious thing to knock a king down with a trunk and land on his head yourself the minute he gets up again," sighed the sprite.

"But didn't you tell me your parents were unfairies?" put in Jimmieboy, eying the sprite distrustfully.

"Yes; but they were only my adopted parents," explained the sprite. "They were a very rich old couple with lots of money and no children, so I adopted them not knowing that they were unfairies. When they died they left me all their bad habits, and their money went to found a storeroom for worn out lawn-mowers. That was a sample of their meanness."

"Well that's a pretty good story," said Jimmieboy.

"Yes," said the sprite, with a pleased smile. "And the best part of it is it's all true."

"Tut!" ejaculated the major, scornfully. "Wait until you hear mine."

CHAPTER X.

THE MAJOR'S TALE.

"A GREAT many years ago when I was a souvenir spoon," said the major, "I belonged to a very handsome and very powerful potentate."

"I didn't quite understand what it was you said you were," said the sprite, bending forward as if to hear better.

"At the beginning of my story I was a souvenir spoon," returned the major.

"Did you begin your career as a spoon?" asked the sprite.

"I did not, sir," replied the major. "I began my career as a nugget in a lead mine where I was found by the king of whom I have just spoken, and on his return home with me he gave me to his wife who sent me out to a lead smith's and had me made over into a souvenir spoon— and a mighty handsome spoon I was too. I had a poem engraved on me that said:

'Aka majo te roo li sah,
Pe mink y rali mis tebah.'

"Rather pretty thought, don't you think so?" added the major as he completed the couplet.

"Very!" said the sprite, with a knowing shake of his head.

"Well, I don't understand it at all," said Jimmieboy.

"Ask this native of Twinkleville what it means," observed the major with a snicker. "He says it's a pretty thought, so of course he understands it—though I assure you I don't, for it doesn't mean anything. I made it up, this very minute."

The sprite colored deeply. It was quite evident that he had fallen into the trap the major had set for him.

"I was only fooling," he said, with a sickly attempt at a smile. "Go on with your story."

"I think perhaps the happiest time of my life was during the hundreds of years that I existed in the royal museum as a spoon," resumed the major. "I was brought into use only on state occasions. When the King of Mangapore gave a state banquet to other kings in the neighborhood I was the spoon that was used to ladle out the royal broth."

Here the major paused to smack his lips, and then a small tear appeared in one corner of his eye and trickled slowly down the side of his nose.

"I always weep," he said, as soon as he could speak, "when I think of that broth. Here is what it was made of:

'Seven pies of sweetest mince,
Then a ripe and mellow quince,
    Then a quart of tea.
Then a pint of cinnamon,
Next a roasted apple, done
    Brown as brown can be.

Add of orange juice, a gill,
And a sugared daffodil,
    Then a yellow yam.
Sixty-seven strawberries
Should be added then to these,
    And a pot of jam.

Mix with maple syrup and
Let it in the ice-box stand
    Till it's good and cold—
Throw a box of raisins in,
Stir it well—just make it spin—
    Till it looks like gold.'

"Oh, my!" cried the major. "What a dish it was, and I, I used to be dipped into a tureen full of it sixteen times at every royal feast, and before the war we had royal feasts on an average of three times a day."

"Three royal banquets a day?" cried Jimmie-boy, his mouth watering to think of it.

"Yes," returned the major. "Three a day until the unhappy war broke out which destroyed all my happiness, and resulted in the downfall of sixty-four kings."

"How on earth did such a war as that ever happen to be fought?" asked the sprite.

"I am sorry to say," replied the major, sadly, "that I was the innocent cause of it all. It was on the king's birthday that war was declared. He used to have magnificent birthday parties, quite like those that boys like Jimmieboy here have, only instead of having a cake with a candle in it for each year, King Fuzzywuz used to have one guest for each year, and one whole cake for each guest. On his twenty-first birthday he had twenty-one guests; on his thirtieth, thirty, and so on; and at every one of these parties I used to be passed around to be admired, I was so very handsome and valuable."

"Absurd!" said the sprite, with a sneering laugh. "The idea of a lead spoon being valuable!"

"If you had ever been able to get into the society of kings," the major answered, with a great deal of dignity, "you would know that on the table of a monarch lead is much more rare than silver and gold. It was this fact that made me so overpoweringly valuable, and it is not surprising that a great many of the kings who used to come to these birthday parties should become envious of Fuzzywuz and wish they owned a treasure like myself. One very old king died of envy because of me, and his heir-apparent inherited his father's desire to possess me to such a degree that he too pined away and finally disappeared entirely. Just regularly faded out of sight. Didn't die, you know, as you would, but vanished.

"So it went on for years, and finally on his sixty-fourth birthday King Fuzzywuz gave his usual party, and sixty-four of the choicest kings in the world were invited. They every one came, the feast was made ready, and just as the guests took their places around the table, the broth with me lying at the side of the tureen was brought in. The kings all took their crowns off in honor of my arrival, when suddenly pouf! a gust of wind came along and blew out every light in the hall. All was darkness, and in the midst of it I felt myself grabbed by the handle and shoved hastily into an entirely strange pocket,

" 'What, ho, without there!' cried Fuzzywuz. 'Turn off the wind and bring a light.'

"The slaves hastened to do as they were told, and in less time than it takes to tell it, light and order were restored. And then a terrible scene ensued. I could see it very plainly through a button-hole in the cloak of the potentate who had seized me and hidden me in his pocket. Fuzzywuz immediately discovered that I was missing.

" 'What has become of our royal spoon?' he roared to the head-waiter, who, though he was an African of the blackest hue, turned white as a sheet with fear.

" 'It was in the broth, oh, Nepotic Fuzzywuz, King of the Desert and most noble Potentate of the Sand Dunes, when I, thy miserable servant, brought it into the gorgeous banqueting hall and set it here before thee, who art ever my most Serene and Egotistic Master,' returned the slave, trembling with fear and throwing himself flat upon the dining-hall floor.

" 'Caitiff!' cried the king. 'I believe thou hast played me false. Do spoons take wings unto themselves and fly away? Are they tadpoles that they develop legs and hop as frogs from our royal presence? Do spoons evapidate——'

" 'Evaporate, my dear,' suggested the queen in a whisper.

" 'Thanks,' returned the king. 'Do spoons evaporate like water in the sun? Do they raise sails like sloops of war and thunder noiselessly out of sight? No, no. Thou hast stolen it and thou must bear the penalty of thy predilection——'

" 'Dereliction,' whispered the queen, impatiently.

" 'He knows what I mean,' roared the king, 'or if he doesn't he will when his head is cut off.' "

"Is that what all those big words meant?" asked Jimmieboy.

" As I remember the occurrence, it is," returned the major. "What the king really meant was always uncertain; he always used such big words and rarely got them right. Reprehensibility and tremulousness were great favorites of his, though I don't believe he ever knew what they meant. But, to continue my story, at this point the king rose and sharpening the carving knife was about to behead the slave's head off when the potentate who had me in his pocket cried out:

" 'Hold, oh Fuzzywuz! The slave is right. I saw the spoon myself at the side of yon tureen when it was brought hither.'

" 'Then,' returned the king, 'it has been perco-
lated——'

" 'Peculated,' whispered the queen.

" 'That's what I said,' retorted Fuzzywuz,
angrily. 'The spoon has been speculated by some
one of our royal brethren at this board. The point
to be liquidated now is, who has done this deed.
What, ho, without there! A guard about the
palace gates—and lock the doors and bar the windows. We shall have a search. I am sorry to say,
that every king in this room save only myself and
my friend Prince Bigaroo, who at the risk of his
kingly dignity deigned to come to the rescue of
my slave, must repeal—I should say reveal— the
contents of his pockets. Prince Bigaroo must be
innocent or he would not have ejaculated as he
hath.'

"You see," said the major, in explanation,
"Bigaroo having stolen me was smart enough to
see how it would be if he spoke. A guilty person in nine cases out of ten would have kept
silent and let the slave suffer. So Bigaroo escaped; but all the others were searched and
of course I was not found. Fuzzywuz was wild
with sorrow and anger, and declared that unless
I was returned within ten minutes he would
wage war upon, and utterly destroy, every king

in the place. The kings all turned pale—even Bigaroo's cheek grew white, but having me he was determined to keep me and so the war began."

"Why didn't you speak and save the innocent kings?" asked the sprite.

"How could I?" retorted the major. "Did you ever see a spoon with a tongue?"

The sprite made no answer. He evidently had never seen a spoon with a tongue.

"The war was a terrible one," said the major, resuming his story. "One by one the kings were destroyed, and finally only Bigaroo remained, and Fuzzywuz not having found me in the treasures of the others, finally came to see that it was Bigaroo who had stolen me. So he turned his forces toward the wicked monarch, defeated his army, and set fire to his palace. In that fire I was destroyed as a souvenir spoon and became a lump of lead once more, lying in the ruins for nearly a thousand years, when I was sold along with a lot of iron and other things to a junk dealer. He in turn sold me to a ship-maker, who worked me over into a sounding lead for a steamer he had built. On my first trip out I was sent overboard to see how deep the ocean was. I fell in between two huge rocks down on the ocean's bed and was caught, the rope connecting me with the ship snapped, and there I was, twenty thousand fathoms under the sea, lost, as I supposed, forever. The effect of the salt water upon me was very much like that of hair restorer on some people's heads. I began to grow a head of green hair—seaweed some people call it—and to this fact, strangely enough, I owed my escape from the water. A sea-cow who used to graze about where I lay, thinking that I was only a tuft of grass gathered me in one afternoon and swallowed me without blinking, and some time after, the cow having been caught and killed by some giant fishermen, I was found by the wife of one of the men when the great cow was about to be cooked. These giants were very strange people who inhabited an island out in the middle of the Atlantic Ocean, which was gradually sinking into the water with the weight of the people on it, and which has now entirely disappeared. There wasn't one of the inhabitants that was less than one hundred feet tall, and in those days they used to act as light-houses for each other at night. They had but one eye apiece, and when that was open it used to flash just like a great electric light, and they'd take turns at standing up in the middle of the island all night long and turning round and round and round until you'd think they'd drop with dizziness. I staid with these people, I should say, about forty years, when one morning two of the giants got disputing as to which of them could throw a stone the farthest. One of them said he could throw a pebble two thousand miles, and the other said he could throw one all the way round the world. At this the first one laughed and jeered, and to prove that he had told the truth the second grabbed up what he thought was a pebble, but which happened to be me and threw me from him with all his force."

"Did you go all the way around?" queried Jimmieboy.

"Did I? Well, rather. I went around once and a half. And sad to say I killed the giant who threw me," returned the major. "I went around the world so swiftly that when I got back to the island the poor fellow hadn't had time to get out of my way, and as I came whizzing along I struck him in the back, went right through him, and leaving him dead on the island went on again and finally fell into a great gun manufactory in Massachusetts where I was smelted over into a bullet, and sent to the war.

I did lots of work for George Washington. I think I must have killed off half a dozen regiments of his enemies, and between you and me, General Washington said I was his favorite bullet, and added that as long as he had me with him he wasn't afraid of anybody."

Here the major paused a minute to smile at the sprite who was beginning to look a little blue, It was rather plain, the sprite thought, that the major was getting the best of the duel.

"Go on," said Jimmieboy. "What next? How long did you stay with George Washington?"

"Six months," said the major. "I'd never have left him if he hadn't ordered me to do work that I wasn't made for. When a bullet goes to war he doesn't want to waste himself on ducks. I wanted to go after hostile generals and majors and cornet players, and if Mr. Washington had used me for them I'd have hit home every time, but instead of that he took me off duck shooting one day and actually asked me to knock over a miserable wild bird he happened to want. I rebelled at this. He insisted, and I said, 'very well, General, fire away.' He fired, the duck laughed, and I simply flew off into the woods on the border of the bay and rested there for nearly a hundred years. The rest of my story is soon told. I lay where I had fallen until six years ago when I was picked up by a small boy who used me for a sinker to go fishing with, after which I found my way into the smelting pot once more, and on the Fifteenth of November, 1892, I became what I am, Major Blueface, the handsomest soldier, the bravest warrior, the most talented tin poet that ever breathed."

A long silence followed the completion of the major's story. Which of the two he liked the better Jimmieboy could not make up his mind, and he hoped his two companions would be considerate enough not to ask him to decide between them.

"I thought they had to be true stories," said the sprite, gloomily. "I don't think it's fair to tell stories like yours—the idea of your being thrown one and a half times around the world!"

"It's just as true as yours, anyhow," retorted the major, "but if you want to begin all over again and tell another I'm ready for you."

"No," said the sprite. "We'll leave it to Jimmieboy as it is."

"Then I win," said the major.

"I don't know about that, major," said Jimmieboy. "I think you are just about even."

"Do you really think so?" asked the sprite, his face beaming with pleasure.

"Yes," said Jimmieboy. "We'll settle it this way: we'll give five points to the one who told the best, five points to the one who told the longest, and five points to the one who told the shortest story. As the stories are equally good you both get five points for that. The major's was the longest, I think, so he gets five more, but so does the sprite because his was the shortest. That makes you both ten, so you both win."

"Hurrah!" cried the major. "Then I do win."

"Yes," said the sprite, squeezing Jimmieboy's hand affectionately, "and so do I."

Which after all, I think, was the best way to decide a duel of that sort.

CHAPTER XI.

PLANNING A VISIT.

"WELL, now that that is settled," said the major with a sigh of relief, "I suppose we had better start off and see whether Forty-forefoot will attend to this business of getting the provisions for us."

"Yes," said the sprite. "The major is right there, Jimmieboy. You have delayed so long on the way that it is about time you did something, and the only way I know of for you to do it is by getting hold of Fortyforefoot. If you wanted an apple pie and there was nothing in sight but a cart-wheel he would change it into an apple pie for you."

"That's all very well," replied Jimmieboy, "but I'm not going to call on any giant who'd want to eat me. You might just as well understand that right off. I'll try on your invisible coat and if that makes me invisible I'll go. If it doesn't we'll have to try some other plan."

"That is the prudent thing to do," said the major, nodding his approval to the little general. "As my poem tries to teach, it is always wise to use your eyes—or look before you leap. The way it goes is this:

'If you are asked to make a jump,
Be careful lest you prove a gump—
    Awake or e'en in sleep—
Don't hesitate the slightest bit
To show that you've at least the wit
    To look before you leap.

Why, in a dream one night, I thought
A fellow told me that I ought
    To jump to Labrador.
I did not look but blindly hopped,
And where do you suppose I stopped?
    Bang! On my bedroom floor!

I do not say, had I been wise
Enough that time to use my eyes—
    As I've already said—
To Labrador I would have got:
But this *is* certain, I would not
    Have tumbled out of bed.'

"The moral of which is, be careful how you go into things, and if you are not certain that you are coming out all right don't go into them," added the major. "Why, when I was a mouse——"

"Oh, come, major—you couldn't have been a

mouse," interrupted the sprite. "You've just told us all about what you've been in the past, and you couldn't have been all that and a mouse too."

"So I have," said the major, with a smile. "I'd forgotten that, and you are right, too. I couldn't have been a mouse. I should have put what I was going to say differently. If I had ever been a mouse—that's the way it should be—if I had ever been a mouse and had been foolish enough to stick my head into a mouse-trap after a piece of cheese without knowing that I should get it out again, I should not have been here to-day, in all likelihood. Therefore the general is right. Try on the invisible coat, Jimmieboy, and let's see how it works before you risk calling on Fortyforefoot."

"Here it is," said the sprite, holding out his hands with apparently nothing in them.

Jimmieboy laughed a little, it seemed so odd to have a person say "here it is" and yet not be able to see the object referred to. He reached out his hand, however, to take the coat, relying upon the sprite's statement that it was there, and was very much surprised to find that his hand did actually touch something that felt like a coat, and in fact was a coat, though entirely invisible.

"Shall I help you on with it?" asked the major.

"Perhaps you'd better," said Jimmieboy. "It feels a little small for me."

"That's what I was afraid of," said the sprite. "You see it covers me all over from head to foot —that is the coat covers all but my head and the hood covers that—but you are very much taller than I am."

Here Jimmieboy, having at last got into the coat and buttoned it about him, had the strange sensation of seeing all of himself disappear excepting his head and legs. These remaining uncovered were of course still in sight.

"Ha-ha-ha!" laughed the major, merrily, as Jimmieboy walked around. "That is the most ridiculous thing I ever saw. You're nothing but a head and pair of legs."

Jimmieboy smiled and placed the hood over his head and the major roared louder than ever.

"Ha-ha-ha-ha!" he cried. "Oh, my—oh, dear! That's funnier still—now you're nothing but a pair of legs. Hee-hee-hee! Take it off quick or I'll die with laughter."

Jimmieboy took off the hood.

"I'm afraid it won't do, Spritey," he said. "Fortyforefoot would see my legs and if he caught them I'd be lost."

"That's a fact," said the sprite, thoughtfully. "The coat is almost two feet too short for you."

"It's more than two feet too short," laughed the major. "It's two whole legs too short."

"This is no time for joking," said the sprite. "We've too much to talk about to use our mouths for laughing."

"All right," said the major. "I won't get off any more, or if I do they won't be the kind to make you laugh. They will be sad jokes—like yours. But I say, boys," he added, "I have a scheme. It is of course the scheme of a soldier and may be attended by danger, but if it is successful all the more credit to the one who succeeds. We three people can attack Fortyforefoot openly, capture him, and not let him go until he provides us with the provisions."

"That sounds lovely," sneered the sprite. "But I'd like to know some of the details of this scheme. It is easy enough to say attack him, capture him and not let him go, but the question is, how shall we do all this?"

"It ought to be easy," returned the major. "There are only three things to be done. The first is to attack him. That certainly ought to be easy. A kitten can attack an elephant if it wants to. The second is to capture him, which, while it seems hard, is not really so if the attack is properly made. The third is not to let him go."

"Clear as a fog," put in the sprite. "But go on."

"Now there are three of us — Jimmieboy, Spriteyboy and Yourstrulyboy," continued the major, "so what could be more natural than that we should divide up these three operations among us? Nothing! Therefore I propose that Jimmieboy here shall attack Fortyforefoot; the sprite shall capture him and throw him into a dungeon cell and I will crown the work by not letting him go."

"Magnificent!" said the sprite. "Jimmieboy and I take all the danger I notice."

""Yes," returned the major. "I am utterly unselfish about it. I am willing to put myself in the background and let you have all the danger and most of the glory. I only come in at the very end—but I don't mind that. I have had glory enough for ten life-times, so why should I grudge you this one little bit of it? My feelings in regard to glory will be found on the fortieth page of Leaden Lyrics or the Ballads of Ben Bullet—otherwise myself. The verses read as follows:

'Though glory, it must be confessed,
　Is satisfying stuff,
Upon my laurels let me rest
　For I have had enough.

Ne'er was a glorier man than I,
　Ne'er shall a glorier be,
Than, trembling reader, you'll espy—
　When haply you spy me.

So bring no more—for while 'tis good
　To have, 'tis also plain
A bit of added glory would
　Be apt to make me vain.'

"And I don't want to be vain," concluded the major.

"Well, I don't want any of your glory," said the sprite, "and if I know Jimmieboy I don't think he does either. If you want to reverse your order of things and do the dangerous part of the work yourself, we will do all in our power to make your last hours comfortable, and I will see to it that the newspapers tell how bravely you died, but we can't go into the scheme any other way."

"You talk as if you were the general's prime minister, or his nurse," retorted the major, "whereas in reality I, being his chief of staff, am they if anybody are."

Here the major blushed a little because he was

not quite sure of his grammar. Neither of his companions seemed to notice the mixture, however, and so he continued:

"General, it is for you to say. Shall my plan go or shall she stay?"

"Well, I think myself, major, that it is a little too dangerous for me, and if any other plan could be made I'd like it better," answered Jimmieboy, anxious to soothe the major's feelings which were evidently getting hurt again. "Suppose I go back and order the soldiers to attack Forty-forefoot and bring him in chains to me?"

"Couldn't be done," said the sprite. "The minute the chains were clapped on him he would change them into doughnuts and eat them all up."

"Yes," put in the major, "and the chances are he would turn the soldiers into a lot of toy balloons on a string and then cut the string."

"He couldn't do that," said the sprite, "because he can't turn people or animals into anything. His power only applies to things."

"Then what shall we do?" said Jimmieboy, in despair.

"Well, I think the best thing to do would be for me to change myself into a giant bigger than he is," said the sprite. "Then I could put you and the major in my pockets and call upon Forty-

forefoot and ask him, in a polite way, to turn
some pebbles and sticks and other articles into
the things we want, and, if he won't do it except
he is paid, we'll pay him if we can."

"What do you propose to pay him with?"
asked the major. "I suppose you'll hand him
half a dozen checkerberries and tell him if he'll
turn them into ten one dollar bills he'll have ten
dollars. Fine way to do business that."

"No," said the sprite, mildly. "You can't
tempt Fortyforefoot with money. It is only by
offering him something to eat that we can hope
to get his assistance."

"Ah? And you'll request him to turn a handful of pine cones into a dozen turkeys on toast,
I presume?" asked the major.

"I shall do nothing of the sort. I shall simply
offer to let him have you for dinner—you will
serve up well in croquettes—Blueface croquettes
—eh, Jimmieboy?" laughed the sprite.

The poor major turned white with fear and
rage. At first he felt inclined to slay the sprite
on the spot, and then it suddenly flashed across
his mind that before he could do it the sprite
might really turn himself into a giant and do
with him as he had said. So he contented himself
with turning pale and giving a sickly smile.

"That would be a good joke on me," he said. "But really, my dear Mr. Sprite, I don't think I would enjoy it, and after all I have a sort of notion that I would disagree with Forty-forefoot—which would be extremely unfortun-ate. I know I should rest like lead on his diges-tion—and that would make him angry with you and I should be sacrificed for nothing."

"Well, I wouldn't consent to that anyhow," said Jimmieboy. "I love the major too much to——"

"So do we all," interrupted the sprite. "Why even I love the major and I wouldn't let anybody eat him for anything—no, sir!—not if I were offered a whole vanilla éclaire would I permit the major to be eaten. But my scheme is the only one possible. I will turn myself into a giant twice as big as Fortyforefoot; I will place you and the major in my pockets and then I will call upon him. He will be so afraid of me that he will do almost anything I ask him to, but to make him give us the very best things he can make I would rather deal gently with him, and instead of forcing him to make the peaches and cherries I'll offer to trade you two fellows off for the things we need. He will be pleased enough at the chance to get anything so good to eat as you look, and he'll prepare everything for us, and he will put you down stairs in the pantry. Then I will tell him stories, and some of the major's jokes, to make him sleepy, and when finally he dozes off I will steal the pantry key and set you free. How does that strike you, general?"

"It's a very good plan unless Fortyforefoot should find us so toothsome looking that he would want to eat us raw. We may be nothing more than fruit for him, you know, and truly I don't want to be anybody's apple," said Jimmieboy.

"You are quite correct there, general," said the major, with a chuckle. "In fact, I'm quite sure he'd think you and I were fruit because being two we are necessarily a pear."

"It won't happen," said the sprite. "He isn't likely to think you are fruit and even if he does I won't let him eat you. I'll keep him from doing it if I have to eat you myself."

"Oh, of course, then, with a kind promise like that there is nothing left for us to do but accept your propostion," said the major. "As Ben Bullet says:

> 'When only one thing can be done—
> If people only knew it—
> The wisest course beneath the sun
> Is just to go and do it.' "

"I'm willing to take my chances," said Jimmieboy, "if after I see what kind of a giant you can turn yourself into I think you are terrible enough to frighten another giant."

"Well, just watch me," said the sprite, taking off his coat. "And mind, however terrifying I may become, don't you get frightened, because I won't hurt you."

"Go ahead," said the major, valiantly. "Wait until we get scared before talking like that to us."

"One, two, three!" cried the sprite. "Presto! Change!

'Bazam, bazam,
A sprite I am,
Bazoo, bazee,
A giant I'd be.'"

Then there came a terrific noise; the trees about the little group shook to the very last end of their roots, all grew dark as night, and as quickly grew light again. In the returning light Jimmieboy saw looming up before him a fearful creature, eighty feet high, clad in a magnificent suit embroidered with gold and silver, a fierce mustache upon his lip, and dangling at his side was a heavy sword.

It was the sprite now transformed into a giant —a terrible-looking fellow, though to Jimmieboy he was not terrible because the boy knew that the dreadful creature was only his little friend in disguise.

"How do I look?" came a bellowing voice from above the trees.

"First rate. Horribly frightful. I'm sure you'll do, and I am ready," said Jimmieboy, with a laugh. "What do you think, major?"

But there came no answer, and Jimmieboy, looking about him to see why the major made no reply, was just in time to see that worthy soldier's coat-tails disappearing down the road.

The major was running away as fast as he could go.

CHAPTER XII.

IN FORTYFOREFOOT VALLEY.

"YOU'VE frightened him pretty well, Spritey," said Jimmieboy, with a laugh, as the major passed out of sight.

"Yes," returned the sprite. "But you don't seem a bit afraid."

"I'm not—though I think I should be if I didn't know who you are," returned Jimmieboy. "You are really a pretty hideous affair."

"Well, I need to be if I am to get the best of Fortyforefoot, but, I say, you mustn't call me Spritey now that I am a giant. It won't do to call me by any name that would show Forty-forefoot who I really am," said the sprite, with a warning shake of his head.

"But what shall I call you?" asked Jimmieboy.

"Bludgeonhead is my name now," replied the sprite. "Benjamin B. Bludgeonhead is my full name, but you know me well enough to call me plain Bludgeonhead."

"All right, plain Bludgeonhead," said Jimmieboy, "I'll do as you say—and now don't you think we'd better be starting along?"

"Yes," said Bludgeonhead, reaching down and grabbing hold of Jimmieboy with his huge hand. "We'll start right away, and until we come in sight of Fortyforefoot's house I think perhaps you'll be more comfortable if you ride on my shoulder instead of in my coat-pocket."

"Thank you very much," said Jimmieboy, as Bludgeonhead lifted him up from the ground and set him lightly as a feather on his shoulder. "My, what a view!" he added, as he gazed about him. "I think I'd like to be as tall as this all the time, Bludgeonhead. What a great thing it would be on parade days to be as tall as this. Why I can see miles and miles of country from here."

"Yes, it's pretty fine—but I don't think I'd care to be so tall always," returned Bludgeon-head, as he stepped over a great broad river that lay in his path. "It makes one very uppish to be as high in the air as this; and you'd be all the time looking down on your friends, too, which would be so unpleasant for your friends that they wouldn't have anything to do with you after a while. Hang on tight now. I'm going to jump over this mountain in front of us."

Here Bludgeonhead drew back a little and then took a short run, after which he leaped high in the air, and he and Jimmieboy sailed easily over the great hills before them, and then alighted safe and sound on the other side.

"That was just elegant!" cried Jimmieboy, clapping his hands with glee. "I hope there are lots more hills like that to be jumped over."

"No, there aren't," said Bludgeonhead, "but if you like it so much I'll go back and do it again."

"Let's," said Jimmieboy.

Bludgeonhead turned back and jumped over the mountain half a dozen times until Jimmieboy was satisfied and then he resumed his journey.

"This," he said, after trudging along in silence for some time, "this is Fortyforefoot Valley, and in a short time we shall come to the giant's castle; but meanwhile I want you to see what a wonderful place this is. The valley itself will give you a better idea of Fortyforefoot's great power as a magician than anything else that I know of. Do you know what this place was before he came here?"

"No," said Jimmieboy. "What was it?"

"It was a great big hole in the ground," returned Bludgeonhead. "A regular sand pit.

Fortyforefoot liked the situation because it was surrounded by mountains and nobody ever wanted to come here because sand pits aren't worth visiting. There wasn't a tree or a speck of a green thing anywhere in sight—nothing but yellow sand glaring in the sun all day and sulking in the moon all night."

"Why how could that be? It's all covered with beautiful trees and gardens and brooks now," said Jimmieboy, which was quite true, for the Fortyforefoot Valley was a perfect paradise to look at, filled with everything that was beautiful in the way of birds and trees and flowers and water courses. "How could he make the trees and flowers grow in dry hot sand like that?"

"By his magic power, of course," answered Bludgeonhead. "He filled up a good part of the sand pit with stones that he found about here, and then he changed one part of the desert into a pond so that he could get all the water he wanted. Then he took a square mile of sand and changed every grain of it into blades of grass. Other portions he transformed into forests until finally simply by the wonderful power he has to change one thing into another he got the place into its present shape."

"But the birds, how did he make them?" asked the little general.

"He didn't," said Bludgeonhead. "They came of their own accord. They saw what a beautiful place this was and they simply moved in."

Bludgeonhead paused a moment in his walk and set Jimmieboy down on the ground again.

"I think I'll take a rest here before going on. We are very near to Fortyforefoot's castle now," he said. "I'll sit down here for a few moments and sharpen my sword and get in good shape for a fight if one becomes necessary. Don't wander away, Jimmieboy. This place is full of traps for just such fellows as you who come in here. That's the way Fortyforefoot catches them for dinner."

So Jimmieboy staid close by Bludgeonhead's side and was very much entertained by all that went on around him. He saw the most wonderful birds imaginable. and great bumble-bees buzzed about in the flowers gathering honey by the quart. Once a great jack-rabbit, three times as large as he was, came rushing out of the woods toward him, and Jimmieboy on stooping to pick up a stone to throw at Mr. Bunny to frighten him away, found that all the stones in that enchanted valley were pre-

cious. He couldn't help laughing outright
when he discovered that the stone he had
thrown at the rabbit was a huge diamond as
big as his fist, and that even had he stopped to
choose a less expensive missile he would have
had to confine his choice to pearls, rubies, emer-
alds, and other gems of the rarest sort. And
then he noticed that what he thought was a rock
upon which he and Bludgeonhead were sitting
was a massive nugget of pure yellow gold. This
lead him on to inspect the trees about him and
then he discovered a most absurd thing. Fortyforefoot's extravagance had prompted him to
make all his pine trees of the most beautifully
polished and richly inlaid mahogany; every one
of the weeping willows was made of solid oak,
ornamented and carved until the eye wearied of
its beauty, and as for the birds in the trees, their
nests were made not of stray wisps of straw and
hay stolen from the barns and fields, but of the
softest silk, rich in color and lined throughout
with eiderdown, the mere sight of which could
hardly help being restful to a tired bird—or boy
either, for that matter, Jimmieboy thought.

"Did he make all this out of sand? All these
jewels and magnificent carvings?" he asked.

"Yes," said Bludgeonhead. "Simply took up a

handful of sand and tossed it up in the air and whatever he commanded it to be it became. But the most wonderful thing in this place is his spring. He made what you might call a 'Wish Dipper' out of an old tin cup. Then he dug a hole and filled it with sand which he commanded to become liquid, and, when the sand heard him say that, it turned to liquid, but the singular thing about it is that as Fortyforefoot didn't say what kind of liquid it should be, it became any kind. So now if any one is thirsty and wants a glass of cider all he has to do is to dip the wish dipper into the spring and up comes cider. If he wants lemonade up comes lemonade. If he wants milk up comes milk. It's simply great."

As Bludgeonhead spoke these words Jimmieboy was startled to hear something very much like an approaching footstep far down the road.

"Did you hear that?" he asked, seizing Bludgeonhead by the hand.

"Yes, I did," replied Bludgeonhead, in a whisper. "It sounded to me like Fortyforefoot's step, too."

"I'd better hide, hadn't I?" said Jimmieboy.

"Yes," said Bludgeonhead. "Come here and be quick about it. Climb inside my coat and snuggle down out of sight in my pocket. We musn't let him see you yet awhile."

Jimmieboy did as he was commanded, and found the pocket a very comfortable place, only it was a little stuffy.

"It's pretty hot in here," he whispered.

"Well, look up on the left hand corner of the outer side of the pocket and you'll find two flaps that are buttoned up," replied Bludgeonhead, softly. "Unbutton them. One will let in all the air you want, and the other will enable you to peep out and see Fortyforefoot without his seeing you."

In a minute the buttons were found and the flaps opened. Everything happened as Bludgeonhead said it would, and in a minute Jimmieboy, peering out through the hole in the cloak, saw Fortyforefoot approaching.

The owner of the beautiful valley seemed very angry when he caught sight of Bludgeonhead sitting on his property, and hastening up to him, he cried:

"What business have you here in the Valley of Fortyforefoot?"

Jimmieboy shrank back into one corner of the pocket, a little overcome with fear. Fortyforefoot was larger and more terrible than he thought,

"I am not good at riddles," said Bludgeon-head, calmly. "That is at riddles of that sort. If you had asked me the difference between a duck and a garden rake I should have told you that a duck has no teeth and can eat, while a rake has plenty of teeth and can't eat. But when you ask me what business I have here I am forced to say that I can't say."

"You are a very bright sort of a giant," sneered Fortyforefoot.

"Yes," replied Bludgeonhead. "The fact is I can't help being **bright**. My mother polishes me every morning with a damp chamois."

"Do you know to whom you are speaking?" asked Fortyforefoot, threateningly.

"No; not having been introduced to you, I can't say I know you," returned Bludgeonhead. "But I think I can guess. You are Anklehigh, the Dwarf."

At this Fortyforefoot turned purple with rage.

"Anklehigh the Dwarf?" he roared. "I'll right quickly teach thee a lesson thou rash fellow."

Fortyforefoot strode up close to Bludgeonhead, whose size he could not have guessed because Bludgeonhead had been sitting down all this time and was pretty well covered over by his cloak.

BLUDGEONHEAD SHOWS JIMMIEBOY TO FORTYFOREFOOT.   PAGE 174.

"I'll take thee by thine ear and toss thee to the moon," he cried, reaching out his hand to make good his word.

"Nonsense, Anklehigh," returned Bludgeonhead, calmly. "Don't be foolish. No dwarf can fight with a giant of my size."

"But I am not the dwarf Anklehigh," shrieked Fortyforefoot. "I am Fortyforefoot."

"And I am Bludgeonhead," returned the other, rising and towering way above the owner of the valley.

"Mercy sakes!" cried Fortyforefoot, falling on his knees in abject terror. "He'd make six of me! Pardon, O, Bludgeonhead. I did not know you when I was so hasty as to offer to throw you to the moon. I thought you were—er—that you were—er——"

"More easily thrown," suggested Bludgeonhead.

"Yes—yes—that was it," stammered Fortyforefoot. "And now, to show that you have forgiven me, I want you to come to my castle and have dinner with me."

"I'll be very glad to," replied Bludgeonhead. "What are you going to have for dinner?"

"Anything you wish," said Fortyforefoot. "I was going to have a very plain dinner to-night because for to-morrow's dinner I have invited my brother Fortythreefoot and his wife Fortytwoinch to have a little special dish I have been so fortunate as to secure."

"Ah?" said Bludgeonhead. "And what is that dish, pray?"

"Oh, only a sniveling creature I caught in one of my traps this afternoon. He was a soldier, and he wasn't very brave about being caught, but I judge from looking at him that he will make good eating," said Fortyforefoot. "I couldn't gather from him who he was. He had on a military uniform, but he behaved less like a warrior than ever I supposed a man could. It seems from his story that he was engaged upon some secret mission, and on his way back to his army, he stumbled over and into one of my game traps where I found him. He begged me to let him go, but that was out of the question. I haven't had a soldier to eat for four years, so I took him to the castle, had him locked up in the ice-box, and to-morrow we shall eat him."

"Did he tell you his name?" asked Bludgeon-head, thoughtfully.

"He tried to but didn't succeed. He told me so many names that I didn't believe he really owned any of them," said Fortyforefoot. "All I could really learn about him was that he was as brave as a lion, and that if I would spare him he would write me a poem a mile long every day of my life."

"Very attractive offer, that," said Bludgeon-head, with a smile.

"Yes; but I couldn't do it. I wouldn't miss eating him for anything," replied Fortyforefoot, smacking his lips, hungrily. "I'd give anything anybody'd ask, too, if I could find another as good."

"Would you, honestly?" asked Bludgeonhead. "Well, now, I thought you would, and that is really what I have come here for. I have in my pocket here a real live general that I have cap-tured. Now between you and me, I don't eat generals. I don't care for them—they fight so. I prefer preserved cherries and pickled peaches and—er—strawberry jam and powdered sugar and almonds, and other things like that, you know, and it occurred to me that if I let you have the general you would supply me with what I needed of the others."

"You have come to the right place, Bludgeon-head," said Fortyforefoot, eagerly. "I'll give you a million cans of jam, all the pickled peaches and other things you can carry if this general you speak about is a fine specimen,"

"Well, here he is," said Bludgeonhead, hauling Jimmieboy out of his pocket—whispering to Jimmieboy at the same time not to be afraid because he wouldn't let anything happen to him, and so of course Jimmieboy felt perfectly safe, though a little excited.

"Beautiful!" cried Fortyforefoot. "Superb! Got any more?"

"No," answered Bludgeonhead, putting Jimmieboy back into his pocket again. "If I ever do find another, though, you shall have him."

This of course put Fortyforefoot in a tremendously good humor, and before an hour had passed he had not only transformed pebbles and twigs and leaves of trees and other small things into the provisions that the tin soldiers needed, but he had also furnished horses and wagons enough to carry them back to headquarters, and then Fortyforefoot accompanied by Bludgeonhead entered the castle, where the proprietor demanded that Jimmieboy should be given up to him.

Bludgeonhead handed him over at once, and ten minutes later Jimmieboy found himself locked up in the pantry.

Hardly had he time to think over the strange events of the afternoon when he heard a noise in the ice-box over in one corner of the pantry, and on going there to see what was the cause of it he heard a familiar voice repeating over and over again these mournful lines:

"From Giant number one I ran—
  But O the sequel dire!
I truly left a frying-pan
  And jumped into a fire."

"Hullo in there," whispered Jimmieboy. "Who are you?"

"The bravest man of my time," replied the voice in the ice-box. "Major Mortimer Carraway Blueface of the 'Jimmieboy Guards.'"

"Oh, I am so glad to find you again," cried Jimmieboy, throwing open the ice-box door. "I thought it was you the minute I heard your poetry."

"Ah!" said the major, with a sad smile. "You recognized the beauty of the poem?"

"Not exactly," said Jimmieboy. "But you said you were in the fire when I knew you were in the ice-box, and so of course——"

"Of course," said the major, with a frown. "You remembered that when I say one thing I mean another. Well, I'm glad to see you again, but why did you desert me so cruelly?"

CHAPTER XIII.

THE RESCUE.

FOR a moment Jimmieboy could say nothing, so surprised was he at the major's question. Then he simply repeated it, his amazement very evident in the tone of his voice.

"Why did we desert you so cruelly?"

"Yes," returned the major. "I'd like to know. When two of my companions in arms leave me, the way you and old Spriteyboy did, I think you ought to make some explanation. It was mean and cruel."

"But we didn't desert you," said Jimmieboy. "No such idea ever entered our minds. It was you who deserted us."

"I?" roared the major fiercely.

"Certainly," said Jimmieboy calmly. "You. The minute Spritey turned into Bludgeonhead you ran away just about as fast as your tin legs could carry you—frightened to death evidently."

"Jimmieboy," said the major, his voice husky

with emotion, "any other person than yourself
would have had to fight a duel with me for cast-
ing such a doubt as you have just cast upon my
courage. The idea of me, of I, of myself, Major
Mortimer Carraway Blueface, the hero of a hundred and eighty-seven real sham fights, the most
poetic as well as the handsomest man in the 'Jimmieboy Guards' being accused of running away!
Oh! It is simply dreadful!

> "I've been accused of dreadful things,
> Of wearing copper finger-rings,
> Of eating green peas with a spoon,
> Of wishing that I owned the moon,
> Of telling things that weren't the truth,
> Of having cut no wisdom tooth,
> In times of war of stealing buns,
> And fainting at the sound of guns,
> Yet never dreamed I'd see the day
> When it was thought I'd run away.
> Alack—O—well-a-day—alas !
> That this should ever come to pass !
> Alas—O—well-a-day—alack !
> It knocks me flat upon my back.
> Alas—alack—O—well-a-day !
> It fills me full of sore dismay.
> Aday—alas—O—lack-a-well—"

"Are you going to keep that up forever?"
asked Jimmieboy. "If you are I'm going to get
out. I've heard stupid poetry in this campaign,
but that's the worst yet."

"I only wanted to show you what I could do in the way of a lamentation," said the major. "If you've had enough I'll stop of course; but tell me," he added, sitting down upon a cake of ice, and crossing his legs, "how on earth did you ever get hold of the ridiculous notion that I ran away frightened?"

"How?" ejaculated Jimmieboy. "What else was there to think? The minute the sprite was changed into Bludgeonhead I turned to speak to you, and all I could see of you was your coat-tails disappearing around the corner way down the road."

"And just because my coat-tails behaved like that you put me down as a coward?" groaned the major.

"Didn't you run away?" Jimmieboy asked.

"Of course not," replied the major. "That is, not exactly. I hurried off; but not because I was afraid. I was simply going down the road to see if I couldn't find a looking-glass so that Spritey-boy could see how he looked as a giant."

Jimmieboy laughed.

"That's a magnificent excuse," he said.

"I thought you'd think it was," said the major, with a pleased smile. "And when I finally found that there weren't any mirrors to be had along the road I went back, and you two had gone and left me."

"And what did you do then?" asked Jimmie-boy.

"I wrote a poem on sleep. It's a great thing, sleep is, and I wrote the lines off in two tenths of a fifth of a second. As I remember it, this is the way they went:

SLEEP.

"Deserted by my friends I sit,
    And silently I weep,
Until I'm wearied so by it,
I lose my little store of wit ;
    I nod and fall asleep.

Then in my dreams my friends I spy—
    Once more are they my own.
I cease to murmur and to cry,
For then 'tis sure to be that I
    Forget I am alone.

'Tis hence I think that sleep's the best
    Of friends that man has got—
Not only does it bring him rest
But makes him feel that he is blest
    With blessings he has not.'"

"Why didn't you go to sleep if you felt that way?" said Jimmieboy.

"I wanted to find you and I hadn't time. There was only time for me to scratch that poem off on my mind and start to find you and Bludgeyboy," replied the major.

"His name isn't Bludgeyboy," said Jimmieboy, with a smile. "It's Bludgeonhead."

"Oh, yes, I forgot," said the major. "It's a good name, too, Bludgeonpate is."

"How did you come to be captured by Fortyforefoot?" asked Jimmieboy, after he had decided not to try to correct the major any more as to Bludgeonhead's name.

"There you go again!" cried the major, angrily. "The idea of a miserable ogre like Fortyforefoot capturing me, the most sagacitacious soldier of modern times. I suppose you think I fell into one of his game traps?"

"That's what he said," said Jimmieboy. "He said you acted in a very curious way, too—promised him all sorts of things if he'd let you go."

"That's just like those big, bragging giants," said the major. "The idea! why he didn't capture me at all. I came here of my own free will and accord."

"What? Down here into this pantry and into the ice-chest? Oh, come now, major. You can't fool me," said Jimmieboy. "That's nonsense. Why should you want to come here?"

"To meet you, of course," retorted the major.

"That's why. I knew it was part of your scheme to come here. You and I were to be put into the pantry and then old Bludgeyhat was to come and rescue us. I was the one to make the scheme, wasn't I?"

"No. It was Bludgeonhead," said Jimmieboy, who didn't know whether to believe the major or not.

"That's just the way," said the major, indignantly, "he gets all the credit just because he's big and I don't get any, and yet if you knew of all the wild animals I've killed to get here to you, how I met Fortyforefoot and bound him hand and foot and refused to let him go unless he would permit me to spend a week in his ice-chest, for the sole and only purpose that I wished to meet you again, you'd change your mind mighty quick about me."

"You bound Fortyforefoot? A little two-inch fellow like you?" said Jimmieboy.

"Why not?" asked the major. "Did you ever see me in a real sham battle?"

"No, I never did," said Jimmieboy.

"Well, you'd better never," returned the major, "unless you want to be frightened out of your wits. I have been called the living telescope, sir, because when I begin to fight, in the

fiercest manner possible, I sort of lengthen out
and sprout up into the air until I am taller than
any foe within my reach."

"Really?" queried Jimmieboy, with a puzzled
air about him.

"Do you doubt it?" asked the major.

"Well, I should like to see it once," said Jimmieboy. "Then I might believe it."

"Then you will never believe it," returned the
major, "because you will never see it. I never
fight in the presence of others, sir."

As the major spoke these words a heavy footstep was heard on the stairs.

"What is that?" cried the major, springing to
his feet.

> "I do not ask you for your gold,
>   Nor for an old straw hat
> I simply ask that I be told
>   Oh what, oh what is that?"

"It is a footstep on the stairs," said Jimmieboy.

"Oh, dear! Oh, dear!" moaned the major "If
it is Fortyforefoot all is over for us. This is what
I feared.

> "I was afraid he could not wait,
>   The miserable sinner,
> To serve me up in proper state
>   At his to-morrow's dinner.

Alas, he comes I greatly fear
  In search of Major Me, sir,
And that he'll wash me down with beer
  This very night at tea, sir."

"Oh, why did I come here—why——"

"I shall!" roared a voice out in the passage-way.

"You shall not," roared another voice, which Jimmieboy was delighted to recognize as Bludgeonhead's.

"I am hungry," said the first voice, "and what is mine is my own to do with as I please. I shall eat both of them at once. Stand aside!"

"I will toss you into the air, my dear Fortyforefoot," returned Bludgeonhead's voice, "if you advance another step; and with such force, sir, that you will never come down again·"

"Tut, tut! I am not so easily tossed. Stand aside," roared the voice of Fortyforefoot.

The two prisoners in the pantry heard a tremendous scuffling, a crash, and a loud laugh.

Then Bludgeonhead's voice was heard again.

"Good-by, Fortyforefoot," it cried.

"I hope he is not going to leave us," whispered Jimmieboy, but the major was too frightened to speak, and he trembled so that half a dozen times he fell off the ice-cake that he had been sitting on.

"Give my love to the moon when you pass her, and when you get up into the milky way turn half a million of the stars there into baked apples and throw 'em down to me," called Bludgeonhead's voice.

"If you'll only lasso me and pull me back I'll do anything you want me to," came the voice of Fortyforefoot from some tremendous height, it seemed to Jimmieboy.

"Not if I know it," replied Bludgeonhead, with a laugh. "I think I'd like to settle down here myself as the owner of Fortyforefoot Valley. Good-bye."

Whatever answer was made to this it was too indistinct for Jimmieboy to hear, and in a minute the key of the pantry door was turned, the door thrown open, and Bludgeonhead stood before them.

"You are free," he said, grasping Jimmieboy's hand and squeezing it affectionately. "But I had to get rid of him. It was the only way to do it. He wanted to eat you right away."

"And did you really throw him off into the air?" asked Jimmieboy, as he walked out into the hall.

"Yes," said Bludgeonhead. "See that hole in the roof?" he added, pointing upward.

"My!" ejaculated Jimmieboy, as he glanced upward and saw a huge rent in the ceiling, through which, gradually rising and getting smaller and smaller the further he rose, was to be seen the unfortunate Fortyforefoot. "Did he go through there?"

"Yes," replied Bludgeonhead. "I simply picked him up and tossed him over my head. He'll never come back. I shall turn myself into Fortyforefoot and settle down here forever, only instead of being a bad giant I shall be a good one—but hallo! Who is this?"

The major had crawled out of the ice-chest and was now trying to appear calm, although his terrible fright still left him trembling so that he could hardly speak.

"It is Major Blueface," said Jimmieboy, with a smile.

"Oh!" cried Bludgeonhead. "He was Forty-forefoot's other prisoner."

"N—nun—not at—t—at—at all," stammered the major. "I def—fuf—feated him in sus—single combat."

"But what are you trembling so for now?" demanded Bludgeonhead.

"I—I am—m not tut—trembling" retorted the major. "I—I am o—only sh—shivering with—th

—the—c—c—c—cold. I—I—I've bub—been in th—that i—i—i—ice bu—box sus—so long."

Jimmieboy and Bludgeonhead roared with laughter at this. Then giving the major a warm coat to put on they sent him up stairs to lie down and recover his nerves.

After the major had been attended to, Bludgeonhead changed himself back into the sprite again, and he and Jimmieboy sauntered in and out among the gardens for an hour or more and were about returning to the castle for supper when they heard sounds of music. There was evidently a brass band coming up the road. In an instant they hid themselves behind a tree, from which place of concealment they were delighted two or three minutes later to perceive that the band was none other than that of the "Jimmieboy Guards," and that behind it, in splendid military form, appeared Colonel Zinc followed by the tin soldiers themselves.

"Hurrah!" cried Jimmieboy, throwing his cap into the air.

"Ditto!" roared the sprite.

"The same!" shrieked the colonel, waving his sword with delight, and commanding his regiment to halt, as he caught sight of Jimmieboy.

"Us likewise!" cheered the soldiers: following

BLUDGEONHEAD COMES TO THE RESCUE.   PAGE 187.

which came a trembling voice from one of the castle windows which said:

"I also wish to add my cheer
Upon this happy day ;
And if you'll kindly come up here
You'll hear me cry 'Hoor..y.'"

"It's Major Blueface's voice!" cried the colonel. "Is the major ill?"

"No," said the sprite, motioning to Jimmieboy not to betray the major. "Only a little worn-out by the fight we have had with Fortyforefoot."

"With Fortyforefoot?" echoed the colonel.

"Yes," said the sprite, modestly. "We three have got rid of him at last."

"Then the victory is won!" cried the colonel. "Do you know who Fortyforefoot really was?"

"No; who?" asked Jimmieboy, his curiosity aroused.

"The Parallelopipedon himself," said the colonel. "We found that out last night, and fearing that he might have captured our general and our major we came here to besiege him in his castle and rescue our officers."

"But I don't see how Fortyforefoot could have been the Parallelopipedon," said Jimmieboy. "What would he want to be him for, when all he had to do to get anything he wanted was to take sand and turn it into it?"

"Ah, but don't you see," explained the colonel, "there was one thing he never could do as Forty-forefoot. The law prevented him from leaving this valley here in any other form than that of the Parallelopipedon. He didn't mind his confinement to the valley very much at first, but after a while he began to feel cooped up here, and then he took an old packing box and made it look as much like a living Parallelopipedon as he could. Then he got into it whenever he wanted to roam about the world. Probably if you will search the castle you will find the cast-off shell he used to wear, and if you do I hope you will destroy it, because it is said to be a most horrible spectacle—frightening animals to death and causing every flower within a mile to wither and shrink up at the mere sight of it."

"It's all true, Jimmieboy," said the sprite. "I knew it all along. Why, he only gave us those cherries and peaches there in exchange for yourself because he expected to get them all back again, you know."

"It was a glorious victory," said the colonel. "I will now announce it to the soldiers."

This he did and the soldiers were wild with joy

when they heard the news, and the band played a hymn of victory in which the soldiers joined, singing so vigorously that they nearly cracked their voices. When they had quite finished the colonel said he guessed it was time to return to the barracks in the nursery.

"Not before the feast," said the sprite. "We have here all the provisions the general set out to get, and before you return home, colonel, you and your men should divide them among you."

So the table was spread and all went happily. In the midst of the feast the major appeared, determination written upon every line of his face. The soldiers cheered him loudly as he walked down the length of the table, which he acknowledged as gracefully as he could with a stiff bow, and then he spoke:

"Gentlemen," he said, "I have always been a good deal of a favorite with you, and I know that what I am about to do will fill you with deep grief. I am going to stop being a man of war. The tremendous victory we have won to-day is the result entirely of the efforts of myself, General Jimmieboy and Major Sprite—for to the latter I now give the title I have borne so honorably for so many years. Our present victory is one of such brilliantly brilliant brilliance that I feel that I may now retire with lustre enough attached to my name to last for millions and millions of years. I need rest, and here I shall take it, in this beautiful valley, which by virtue of our victory belongs wholly and in equal parts to General Jimmieboy, Major Sprite and myself. Hereafter I shall be known only as Mortimer Carraway Blueface, Poet Laureate of Fortyforefoot Hall, Fortyforefoot Valley, Pictureland. As Governor-General of the country we have decided to appoint our illustrious friend, Major Benjamin Bludgeonhead Sprite. General Jimmieboy will remain commander of the forces, and the rest of you may divide amongst yourselves, as a reward for your gallant services, all the provisions that may now be left upon this table. It is all yours. I demand but one condition. That is that you do not take the table. It is of solid mahogany and must be worth a very considerable sum.

> Now let the saddest word be said,
> Now bend in sorrow deep the head.
> Let tears flow forth and drench the dell :
> Farewell, brave soldier boys, farewell."

Here the major wiped his eyes sadly and sat down by the sprite who shook his hand kindly and thanked him for giving him his title of major.

"We'll have fine times living here together," said the sprite.

"Well, rather!" ejaculated the major. "I'm going to see if I can't have myself made over again, too, Spritey. I'll be pleasanter for you to look at. What's the use of being a tin soldier in a place where even the cobblestones are of gold and silver."

"You can be plated any how," said Jimmie-boy.

"Yes, and maybe I can have a platinum sword put in, and a real solid gold head—but just at present that isn't what I want," said the major. "What I am after now is a piece of birthday cake with real fruit raisins in it and strips of citron two inches long, the whole concealed beneath a one inch frosting. Is there any?"

CHAPTER XIV.

HOME AGAIN.

"I DON'T think we have any here," said Jimmieboy, who was much pleased to see the sprite and the major, both of whom he dearly loved, on such good terms. "But I'll run home and see if I can get some."

"Well, we'll all go with you," said the colonel, starting up and ordering the trumpeters to sound the call to arms.

"All except Blueface and myself," said the sprite. "We will stay here and put everything in readiness for your return."

"That is a good idea," said Jimmieboy. "And you'll have to hurry for we shall be back very soon."

This, as it turned out, was a very rash promise for Jimmieboy to make, for after he and the tin soldiers had got the birthday cake and were ready to enter Pictureland once more, they found that not one of them could do it, the frame was so high up and the picture itself so hard and

impenetrable. Jimmieboy felt so badly to be
unable to return to his friends, that, following
the major's hint about sleep bringing forgetful-
ness of trouble, he threw himself down on the
nursery couch, and closing his brimming eyes
dozed off into a dreamless sleep.

It was quite dark when he opened them again
and found himself still on the couch with a piece
of his papa's birthday cake in his hand, his sor-
rows all gone and contentment in their place.
His papa was sitting at his side, and his mamma
was standing over by the window smiling.

"You've had a good long nap, Jimmieboy,"
said she, "and I rather think, from several things
I've heard you say in your sleep, you've been
dreaming about your tin soldiers."

"I don't believe it was a dream, mamma," he
said, "it was all too real." And then he told his
papa all that had happened.

"Well, it is very singular," said his papa, when
Jimmieboy had finished, "and if you want to
believe it all happened you may; but you say all
the soldiers came back with you except Major
Blueface?"

"Yes, every one," said Jimmieboy.

"Then we can tell whether it was true or not
by looking in the tin soldier's box. If the major

isn't there he may be up in Fortyforefoot castle as you say."

Jimmieboy climbed eagerly down from the couch and rushing to the toy closet got out the box of soldiers and searched it from top to bottom. The major was not to be seen anywhere, nor to this day has Jimmieboy ever again set eyes upon him.

THE END.

Reprint Publishing

www.reprintpublishing.com

www.ingramcontent.com/pod-product-compliance
Lightning Source LLC
Chambersburg PA
CBHW051653260626
47170CB00004B/1474